Choose *your* own Ever After

THE Call of the Wild

Choose Your own Ever After

THE Call of the Wild

BY JULIE FISON

Kane Miller

A DIVISION OF EDC PUBLISHING

Chapter One

I could tell as soon as I boarded the bus that the news was big. Very big. I pushed my way down the aisle towards my friends, buzzing with excitement. Kimmi and Annabel were practically dancing in their seats.

"We're in, we're in!" Annabel sang, as I approached.

I dumped my bag on the floor and slid into the seat beside Annabel. "No way!"

"Yes way," she said, smiling. "We're on the guest list."

I stared at Annabel, hardly able to believe my ears. We'd talked about nothing else for the past week, but I'd never really believed that she could pull it off. Until now.

"Ryan Baker's party!" Kimmi said, drumming her hands on my seat. "Pretty cool, right, Phoebs?"

I grinned at her. "Too cool." Apparently, Ryan Baker lived in some kind of mansion right on the harbor. His party would be out of this world. It wasn't the sort of thing Westway girls normally got invited to, but Annabel's neighbor Marco went to Highgrove with Ryan, and he'd gotten us on the guest list.

"Ryan Baker." Annabel sighed and gazed out the window. "At last we meet."

Annabel had been dreaming about Ryan since the start of the year. She'd seen him getting out of his mum's Porsche at Marco's house and had been hooked ever since. She said icicles practically dripped off him, he was that cool. So far she'd just drooled over him from a distance. She followed him on Instagram and stuff, but she'd never gotten close enough to talk to him. The party would be her big chance.

"So, Marco came through after all," I said. "I thought you said he was being tricky?"

"Yep, good ol' Marco," Annabel replied. Her face

suddenly got serious. "But there is a catch."

I frowned. "What's that?"

"He wants us to go over to his house every weekend for the next year. Tidy his room, wash his dirty socks and –" Annabel paused for dramatic effect "– clean the dirt from under his toenails."

"No!" Kimmi yelped and covered her ears. She had a major thing for Annabel's neighbor. "Marco is divinely lovely. He doesn't have dirty toenails."

"Jokes!" Annabel grinned. "I'll probably just have to tell him a million times what a king he is for getting us into the party. But it'll be worth it!"

"For sure," I said, but I was feeling a bit nervous. Now that we were actually invited, I was having second thoughts. While Annabel was off with Ryan and Kimmi was with Marco, who would I hang out with? "You guys aren't going to leave me all alone while you chase after Ryan and Marco, are you?"

"Of course not." Annabel squeezed my arm. "We need you there. And Marco's got heaps of cute friends he can introduce you to."

"Yeah, what about that guy you mentioned," Kimmi asked Annabel. "What was his name?"

"Yes! Saia," Annabel enthused. "I've already told him about you, Phoebs. You'll love him."

"What?" My jaw fell open. "What did you say to him?"

"Nothing. Well, just that you're amazing, and single," Annabel said. "I mean, I know your heart belongs to Bunga the orangutan, but Saia's pretty gorgeous, you know, for an actual … guy."

Kimmi and Annabel giggled. They loved teasing me about how I seemed more interested in animals than guys. I was in the school Wild Club and Bunga was an orphaned orangutan that we sponsored. But he *was* incredibly cute, and I'd rather hang out with an orangutan than most of the boys in our year.

I laughed along with them. "Who are these *cute guy creatures* you speak of?"

"You'll see," Kimmi said. "And you're going to be very pleased you discovered them."

"So, the countdown begins." Annabel rubbed her

hands together. "Eight days till the party!"

I took a deep breath and stared down the aisle, wondering what Saia was like. I hoped I'd like him. I'd never really had a serious crush on anyone before, but Annabel and Kimmi were always talking about their latest obsessions. It would be nice to join in.

Was Saia tall and strong, or short and stocky? Was he loud and funny, or quiet and serious? A little tingle ran up my neck at the thought of finding out.

Chapter Two

By the time we got to school, our excitement levels were off the scale. We'd decided to meet at Kimmi's place before the party to get ready. Afterward, we'd stay at Annabel's, since she lived the closest to Ryan's.

"We can stay up all night!" Annabel said, banging her locker shut.

"For sure," Kimmi agreed. "I don't think I'll be able to sleep anyway, after hanging out with Marco."

"As opposed to hanging out in the tree in my backyard, blowing kisses at him?" Annabel teased.

Kimmi gave Annabel a playful slap on the arm. "I've only done that once."

I laughed. I'd seen her do it at least ten times. She really was crazy about Marco. The last time she'd done it, Marco had actually waved back. Maybe at Ryan's party, they would finally get together!

"It's going to be amazing," Annabel said, looking at her phone. "And guess who just posted an *exclusive* event page?"

I peered over Annabel's shoulder. There it was, the "Ryan Baker Party" page. And there we were, on the guest list. I had to check twice just to make sure. Annabel stroked Ryan's profile picture and then hit the join button.

Kimmi and I pulled out our phones and accepted our invitations as well. Now it was official. I scrolled through the guest list until I found Saia. I clicked on his profile to check out his picture. He looked back at me with lovely brown eyes and a great big smile. He was seriously cute.

"He's hot, right?" Kimmi said, peering at the picture on my screen.

"Yeah, he's not bad," Annabel said, checking out Saia.

"But look how gorgeous Ryan is." She sighed, scrolling through pictures on her phone. "I can't wait for the party."

"So," I said, nudging Annabel. "Do you think you'll get together with him?"

Annabel smiled coyly and kissed a picture of Ryan posing on the beach.

Kimmi winked at Annabel. "How about for real?"

Annabel paused for a moment, and then nodded. We all squealed.

Then a message popped up on my phone.

Saia Natane wants to be your friend.

"Annabel, look at this!"

She grabbed my phone. "Oh! Accept, accept!" she said, pressing accept.

"Annabel!" I shrieked, snatching my phone back.

"Girls!" came a loud voice from the end of the corridor. "I'm sure you have classes to get to." Miss Treemore glared at us. "I expect more from a class representative, Phoebe."

"Yes, Miss Treemore," I said, shoving my phone away. There were distinct disadvantages to having a leadership position.

I grabbed my science book from my locker and we headed off to class, chattering as quietly as possible about what we might wear to the party. Kimmi had just bought a new black crop top. She showed me a photo.

"Wow! You'll look so cute in that," I said.

I showed Kimmi a picture of one of the outfits that I was considering for the party – a little satin green top with black shorts. "What do you think?" I asked.

Kimmi smiled. "You'd look good in anything."

"Really?" I wasn't sure about the top. My little sister, Lulu, had told me to buy it the last time I went shopping with her and Mum.

"Let me have a look," Annabel said. She grabbed my phone and inspected the picture. "*Oh,*" she began. "No offense, but you look a bit like a frog. A cute one, obviously."

I took my phone back, feeling slightly offended. I've got a soft spot for amphibians, especially frogs. But I didn't want to look like one.

Kimmi smiled. "She's just waiting for her prince to come along and turn her into a princess."

"I think it's meant to be the other way around," I said. I deleted the photo. "That's what I get for taking fashion advice from a four year old."

Kimmi gave my shoulder a squeeze. "Keep your little sister away from your clothes."

"I know!" cried Annabel, as if she'd just made some incredible scientific breakthrough. "How about you borrow my pink top with the low back? That would really work with those shorts."

"Really? You don't mind?" I asked.

Annabel was beaming. "Of course not."

I felt excited, just thinking about it. Everything Annabel owned totally rocked. This was all working out perfectly. I just needed to sort out some accessories. And I had all weekend to shop for those!

There was a poster for the Wild Club pinned up on the bulletin board outside the girls' bathroom. The poster showed our sponsored orangutan, Bunga. His big brown eyes stared out at me pleadingly, his head tilted in an impossibly loveable way. The little tufts of red hair that stuck up from the back of his head just made me want to hug him.

Bunga the orangutan needs you!

Join the Wild Club and find out how you can help.

I didn't know how anyone could resist Bunga. I'd signed up for the Wild Club as soon as the poster had appeared. I thought it was so cool that we could sponsor an orphaned orangutan.

"What do you think?" I asked Kimmi when she emerged from the bathroom, flicking water from her hands.

"We should go shopping this afternoon to get our accessories," she said.

"No." I nodded at the poster. "What do you think about joining the Wild Club?"

Kimmi stood back and considered the poster, as if she'd never seen it before. "Cute monkey."

I sighed. "You know he's an orangutan, not a monkey," I said. "But what do you think? Are you going to join?"

The club met every Friday at lunchtime. I'd missed a few meetings lately because of a conflict with debate team, but I was definitely going today.

Kimmi shrugged. "Suppose," she said eventually.

"Really?" I said, not quite believing what I was hearing. I'd been begging Kimmi and Annabel to join for months. I really liked some of the people in the club and I wanted my friends to meet them. And now, finally, Kimmi had agreed to come along. I gave her a big hug. "You won't regret it, I promise. The club is really great. Jack 'n Liam have all kinds of plans to raise money to help save animals."

"Cool," Kimmi nodded, clearly not listening to what I was telling her. But I didn't mind too much. It was enough that she'd agreed to join the club. She could catch up on the details later.

"Don't make plans for lunch," I told Annabel when we saw her in the corridor outside our French class. She was still staring at pictures of Ryan on her phone.

"We're going to save some monkeys," Kimmi said.

"Orangutans," I corrected her. "Kimmi's decided to

join the Wild Club. You have to come, too."

Annabel raised her eyebrows. "Is this about Bunga again?"

I nodded. "Please come. It'll be fun."

"It'll be a bunch of nature nerds," Annabel scoffed. "Any chance of encountering cute, wild males there?"

I smiled to myself. "There are a few cute ones."

"What? Monkeys or actual guys?" Kimmi asked, laughing.

I elbowed Kimmi as Madame Clements popped her head out of the classroom and stared at us.

But Annabel was too busy miming a passionate smooch with a photo of Ryan to notice. "Sorry, Ryan. I've gotta leave you at lunchtime to save some orangutans. Miss you already."

Madame Clements cleared her throat. "*Entrez, s'il vous plaît!* Will you ladies be joining us this morning? Or would you like to stay out there? You can explain to the headmaster why you're kissing your phone in the corridor."

Annabel stuffed her phone away. "Coming, Madame."

We marched single file into the classroom behind another group of stragglers, mumbling a greeting to Madame Clements in French. Class hadn't even started and we were already in trouble, but I didn't care. I couldn't wait to introduce Kimmi and Annabel to my "nature nerd" friends.

Chapter Three

The bell for the end of class and the start of lunchtime came and went and still we sat at our desks, listening to two girls mangle the days of the week in French. I mean, seriously. *Mercredi* and *Vendredi* weren't that hard to remember or pronounce. But now we were all being kept in. We'd be late for the Wild Club meeting.

"Let's all have one more try to get it right," said Madame Clements.

So, off we all went, reciting the days of the week. Once we had been through that ten times, she made us write the words out another ten times before finally letting us leave.

"Glad that's over," Annabel said when we got outside.

"So annoying," I agreed. "I hate being kept in."

Kimmi just groaned. She marched across the quad to the bench where we normally had lunch.

"What are you doing?" I asked, as Kimmi and Annabel sat down. "We're going to the Wild Club, aren't we?"

"Really?" Kimmi whimpered. "That French class fried my brain. I don't think I've got anything left for the monk … orangutans."

Annabel looked pleadingly at me. "Can't we just let this one go? I know you love animals. But I really love a lunch break."

"But you guys said you'd come," I protested. "And you'll really like the others in the club. There are two really great –"

"Okay, okay," Kimmi interrupted. "I'll come."

I gave her a little clap as she got to her feet.

"All right, then," said Annabel. "If you're both going."

"You'll like it!" I grinned. "You know, Jack 'n Liam from the Wild Club went to Borneo last year and visited some orangutans," I said, as we headed towards the meeting. "How cool is that?"

"That's amazing." Kimmi smiled. "Where's Borneo?"

I rolled my eyes. "It's the biggest island in Asia. The bottom is part of Indonesia, the top is Malaysian, and Brunei is in the corner. There are rain forests and beaches – and some very cute orangutans!"

Annabel's eyes sparkled. "Imagine lying on a beach and watching orangutans playing in the trees."

When we arrived at the meeting room, the door was closed. We were so late that the meeting was already underway. This was going to be awkward. I gently turned the door handle, but it didn't budge. "I think it's locked," I whispered. "That's weird."

Annabel nudged me aside. "Probably just stuck. The building's a hundred years old."

She turned the handle and gave the door a shove. Nothing. So she shook it a bit. Still nothing. Looking determined, she turned the handle and shouldered the door, like she was a cop bursting in on the scene of a crime. The door swung open and Annabel flew in. She staggered across the classroom, arms and legs flying

everywhere, finishing up in front of the whiteboard –
with a picture of an orangutan projected on her face.

"Ta-da!" she cried, throwing her arms in the air, like
she'd planned the dramatic entrance. Typical Annabel.

Kimmi snorted. She followed Annabel into the
meeting room, but kept her head down.

"The comedy workshop is two doors down," came
a voice from the back. A ripple of sniggers went through
the room as a girl got to her feet. It was Polly, president
of the Wild Club. She was very, very serious about the
club, and a bit on the scary side.

"I've brought some friends to save Bunga. Sorry
we're late," I said, glancing over at my usual table. Jack
and Liam were both there, smirking at us.

"That's great," Polly said, relaxing. "Just in time to
help out with our next fundraiser."

"Okay!" I smiled as Polly sat down again.

"This is totes awkward," Kimmi whispered. "We
should go."

I shook my head and started walking towards my
usual seat.

"What's this stupid fundraiser?" Annabel muttered under her breath. Then she saw where I was headed. "Oh, wow," she whispered. "You weren't kidding about the cute guys." She sashayed confidently towards Liam and Jack. It was weird. When I first met Liam at the start of the year, I'd definitely noticed him. There was something about his blue eyes that went right through you. And Jack was cute, too, in a quiet way. But they were both in the year above, so they felt a bit out of my league. Since then, we'd become good friends. I guess I'd sort of forgotten about Liam being OMG cute.

"Hey, Phoebe," Liam said, as I sat down next to him. "Long time no see."

"Thought you'd quit the club," Jack added.

I shook my head. "I told you I had debate. Couldn't get out of it. Did you miss me?"

"Of course!" Liam said, and he looked at me, just a little too long, until Annabel cleared her throat.

As I turned to introduce my friends, I couldn't help noticing that they looked a bit dazed. It was as if they'd never seen guys before. Kimmi got tongue-tied when she tried to say hello, and Annabel started giggling about nothing.

"So, you guys like orangutans?" Annabel smiled as she sat down across from Liam. "They're sweet, huh?"

Liam frowned. "Yeah, we like them, but not because they're *sweet*. We're here because they're endangered."

"Right!" I said, cringing at Annabel's clueless comment. "Kimmi and Annabel are really concerned about deforestation and the way it affects wildlife…" I went on with a long list of things I was sure my friends weren't even slightly concerned about.

The way Liam was watching me wasn't making it easy. Why was he being so weird? Everything had been completely fine the last time I came to a Wild Club meeting. Jack had been sick, so Liam and I had sat together and talked about everything *except* orangutans. I'd told Liam all about my crazy family and he'd told me all about his. He had a whole family full of scientists. His parents were marine biologists and his sisters were both studying environmental science. That's when he'd told me about his family trip to Borneo last year, which

Jack had gone on too.

It had been really chill back then, but now Liam seemed ... different. I wondered if bringing Annabel and Kimmi had changed things, or if I'd done something wrong.

Chapter Four

"You should tell Kimmi and Annabel about your trip to Borneo," I said to Jack, trying to shrug off Liam's weirdness.

Liam had told me how they'd stayed in the jungle, rafted down remote rivers and even climbed the highest mountain in Southeast Asia, where they'd seen huge carnivorous plants. It sounded amazing.

"We're actually meant to be sorting out the fund-raiser," Jack said.

"Oh, yeah," I replied. "What's that all about?"

"We're having an outdoor movie night on the school field. *Movie Under the Stars.* We're getting a big screen, and the whole school community's invited."

It's going to be huge," Liam added. "We're having food stands and a raffle and everything. And all the money raised is going towards Bunga's orangutan sanctuary."

"We're in charge of the slushie stand," said Jack.

"Ooh," Annabel said excitedly. "We should call it Slushies in Paradise. And we could give the slushies special names, like Borneo Sunset Orange, Rain Forest Green, Blue Lagoon."

"Yeah." Kimmi nodded. "I could make a big banner and we could hang it from the front of the stand."

"Cool," I said proudly. It was great the way my friends were getting into the idea. They really were going to love the Wild Club after all. I hoped the guys liked their ideas, too.

"Sounds great," Liam said. "But first we need to work out where we're going to get the slushie machines. We haven't sorted that out yet."

I thought for a minute. "Isn't there a slushie place at the mall?" I suggested. "They might be able to help."

"Oh, yeah," Jack said. "Sloppy Slushie. I'm pretty sure they've helped at school events before."

"There's an art shop in the mall, too," Kimmi added. "They might donate some paint for our banner."

"Some shops could donate prizes for the raffle as well," Annabel suggested. "We should all go this afternoon!"

Kimmi and Annabel made plans to meet at the mall with almost as much enthusiasm as they'd talked about the party. It was decided we'd meet at the fountain at 4:30 p.m. Everyone seemed totally psyched about the slushie stand. But I felt a bit strange. I'd gotten to know Liam pretty well since I'd been in the Wild Club, but we'd never done anything outside of school before. For some reason, the idea of hanging out with him at the mall was giving me butterflies.

The bell rang and Polly shouted, "We've got more posters for *Movie Under the Stars* here!" She tapped her hand on a pile at the front of the room. "Put them up everywhere. We need to get the message out. Thanks, guys!"

As I watched Liam strolling towards the door, I tried to work out why I was feeling so nervous about seeing him that afternoon. It was strange. I'd never felt like that about him before.

"Hey, daydreamer," Kimmi said, grabbing my hand. "We need to get some posters before they all go. We can put them up at the mall this afternoon."

"Yeah, right, the mall. We should do that."

Annabel glanced at me. "How long were you going to keep those guys a secret?"

I frowned. "What do you mean? I've told you about them before."

Kimmi shook her head as she picked up a bunch of posters. "You only told us about Jacqueline."

"Huh?" I said. "I've told you about Jack and Liam loads of times."

Annabel laughed. "You must have said *Jack 'n Liam* like one word. We thought you were saying Jacqueline."

I grabbed a pile of posters and handed a stack to Annabel. "So, what do you think of my good friend Jacqueline?" I asked, raising an eyebrow.

"Not too shabby at all," Annabel said.

Kimmi nodded. "*Indeed.* The movie night should be heaps of fun."

And that's when I noticed it. I stopped walking and stared at the posters in my hand. "Has anyone noticed the date for the movie night?"

"Oh no," Kimmi sighed, reading the poster. "I thought it was, like, a month away."

"It's the same night as Ryan Baker's party!" Annabel groaned.

I stared at the poster, hoping it would somehow change if I looked at it hard enough. There had to be something we could do. "Do you think Ryan might change the date for his party?"

Annabel shook her head. "That's not going to happen."

"So which one will we go to?" I asked.

Annabel stared at me. "What do you mean?"

"Well," I began. "On one hand, the party will be epic. But on the other –"

"Phoebs," Kimmi interrupted me. "The party is going to be the best night ever. It's all planned."

"But what about Slushies in Paradise?" I asked.

Annabel frowned. "Since when is making slushies

more fun than going to a party and having a sleepover with your besties?"

"I just think …" But I couldn't quite work out what I thought. The party sounded fun, but I was really only going to keep Annabel and Kimmi company. Would a party with a bunch of guys I didn't know be more fun than making slushies with Liam and Jack?

"What about the thing at the mall this afternoon? We promised Liam –"

"Oh, I get it now," Annabel interrupted. "This isn't about the movie night, is it?"

"What do you mean?" I asked, confused. "What else could it be about?"

Annabel gave me a sly smile. "Liam."

"It's about saving orangutans," I insisted.

"I don't know," said Kimmi. "Liam couldn't take his eyes off you in that meeting. I think he's got a thing for you. And maybe you've got a thing for him too."

"No way," I said, laughing. "Liam and me? That would never happen. We're just friends."

"He's pretty cute," said Annabel.

I shook my head vigorously. "We're friends. That's it. And he's in the year above. We're hardly going to be cozying up under the stars at the movie night."

But even as I said it, I could feel myself blushing at the thought.

"So, you're coming to the party, then?" Kimmi asked.

I shrugged. My head was spinning. I had no idea what to do.

If I went to the party, I'd let down the Wild Club, and poor Bunga. But if I went to the movie night, I'd be letting down my friends. What should I do?

If you think Phoebe should go to Ryan Baker's party, go to page 29.

If you think Phoebe should go to the Wild Club movie night, go to page 81.

Phoebe GOES TO Ryan Baker's *party*

Chapter Five

"You're right," I finally said to Kimmi and Annabel, as we arrived at the mall. It had taken me all afternoon to work out what to do, but I'd made the decision now. "I'll go to the party. I feel bad, but it's not like I've got a contract with the Wild Club."

"Exactly!" said Annabel. "And the party is going to be amazing!"

"We can still help get everything ready and set up the slushie stand," said Kimmi. "We just won't be there to serve slushies on the actual night."

"Ooh, let's look in here for accessories for the party," said Annabel. "It'll only take a minute."

By the time we got to the fountain, we were half an hour late.

"Sorry we're late," I said.

Jack shrugged. "It's cool."

Liam smiled, but he looked tense. He was drumming his fingers on a stack of movie night posters, obviously keen to get on with our mission. I felt guilty that we'd kept them waiting, and I felt even worse that we wouldn't be helping on the slushie stand anymore. I bit my lip, trying to work out how to tell the guys we'd be going to the party instead of the movie night. Liam kept fixing me with an intense look that didn't make it easy.

Annabel didn't seem to notice. "How delicious is this?" She waved the new clutch she'd just bought at Kimmi and me, looking pleased with herself. "I even got a discount."

Liam rolled his eyes and groaned.

"You don't like it?" Annabel said, suddenly noticing Liam's expression.

"I thought we were here to sort out things for the slushie stand," he said.

"Totes," Annabel said, putting her bag away. "I'm ready. And I happen to be a great negotiator. I think you'll be pretty impressed with my skills."

I cringed. Annabel could talk her way into pretty much anything, but she was sounding a bit on the arrogant side.

"Excellent," Liam said. He tucked his posters under his arm. "Let's get started then."

"Before we go …" I took a deep breath "… there's something we need to tell you."

I looked from Liam to Jack, and then glanced at Annabel, hoping she might take over, but she looked away.

"What's up?" Liam asked.

"Well," I hesitated. "We can't actually help at the slushie stand after all."

"You're quitting the Wild Club?" Jack frowned.

"We're not quitting," I said quickly. "We just can't go to the movie night."

Liam scowled. "What are you doing here, then?"

"We still want to help," Kimmi said.

"We'll put up posters and get donations and stuff," I added. "We just can't make it next Saturday."

"Even though that's the actual night of the fundraiser," Liam said, frowning.

I nodded.

"Oh, that makes perfect sense, then," he said sarcastically.

I felt awful. Liam was taking this really badly.

"Why can't you make the movie night?" Jack asked.

"A conflict," Annabel sighed. "We're already committed to a party."

"A party?" Liam looked horrified.

I groaned to myself. This was just getting worse. I suddenly felt completely unreliable, putting a party before my Wild Club responsibilities.

"Not just any party. It's Ryan Baker's party," Annabel went on.

Liam and Jack looked at each other and shrugged. Clearly they had no idea who Ryan Baker was or that he lived in a harborside mansion.

"He goes to Highgrove," Kimmi explained. But that just made things worse.

Liam glared at me. "So, you're going to a party with a bunch of losers from Highgrove instead of coming to the movie night."

"Well, it's not quite like that," I said.

"Yeah," Annabel interrupted. "Highgrove guys aren't losers. They're actually very cute and very charming."

Liam scoffed.

"And we were invited to the party before we found out about the movie night," Annabel went on. "Sorry if that doesn't work for you."

"Whatever," Liam said. "Let's get started. Jack and I will go up to Sloppy Slushie and see if they can help. And you three can … " he shrugged.

"We'll put up posters," I said brightly, even though I was hurt by Liam's tone. "And we'll get some paint and things for the banner. Meet you back here in an hour, okay?"

"Right," Liam said, heading towards the escalator with Jack.

"Happy shopping," Jack called over his shoulder.

I opened my mouth to protest, but they'd gone.

"Wow," Annabel frowned. "Who made them kings of the jungle? Give me a Highgrove guy any day. What is it you like about those guys, Phoebs? They're pretty up themselves for nature nerds."

"They're not normally like that," I said feebly, as the guys disappeared towards the top floor of the mall.

"I guess they're pretty annoyed we're not helping on the slushie stand," Kimmi said.

I felt completely deflated. "I've been in the Wild Club all year, not doing very much. And now, when I'm actually needed, I'm going to a party instead."

Annabel gave me a hug. "You made the right choice. Those guys don't deserve your help. They're lucky we're here at all."

I sighed, pulling a roll of movie night posters out of my schoolbag. "Come on, let's put these up and get the paint and things. Show them we care about more than just shopping and parties."

"Totes," Kimmi said. "The art shop is this way."

We linked arms and marched off down the mall, ready to prove our commitment to the Wild Club.

"I can't believe I thought Liam was kind of cute when I first saw him," Annabel said.

"*Kind of?*" I laughed. "You were practically drooling."

"I thought Jack was pretty sweet too," Kimmi added. "Quiet, but mysterious."

"They're both really nice. But … not so much today."

"They'll get over it," Annabel told me.

I hoped so. It really upset me to think of the guys being mad at me. Especially Liam. I'd thought we were good friends and could talk about anything. "I didn't expect Liam to react *that* badly to us not going to the movie night."

"You know," Kimmi said, "I think Liam might be jealous that you're going to a party with a bunch of Highgrove guys."

I laughed. "Jealous? No way. Mad, yes. But jealous?"

Kimmi nodded. "I told you, he kept looking at you in the meeting today. Didn't he, Annabel?"

She shrugged. "Didn't really notice." She stopped in her tracks as something in a shop window caught her eye. "Hey! That dress. It's just what I've been looking for!"

I sighed as Annabel disappeared into the shop, followed by Kimmi. When Annabel set her mind to something it was pretty hard to divert her. I followed my friends inside, trying not to think about what Liam would say if he could see us.

"It's half price!" Annabel cried, excitedly poring over a white dress.

"It'll totes suit you," Kimmi said.

"Have I got time to try it on?" Annabel asked, looking at me.

I nodded. "Fine, but don't be too long. We've got a stack of things to do before we meet up with the guys again."

Annabel grabbed the dress and then pulled another two from the racks and tucked them under her arm. Then she found another one and handed it to me. "This is *so* you."

I shook my head. I really didn't want to meet the guys with an armful of shopping bags. But Annabel nudged me towards the dressing room, leaving me no choice but to try it on.

"Oh, wow," Kimmi smiled. "That orange is so you. It goes perfectly with your dark hair and eyes."

"You've got to get it for the party," Annabel said.

I looked in the mirror, tilting my head one way and then the other. I did really like it, but there was no way I could get it. "It's cute, but I can't afford it."

Annabel waved a hand. "No problem. I'll lend you the money."

I hesitated. Annabel always seemed to have spare cash and she had no problem sharing it with Kimmi and me. But it didn't feel right, taking her money. I shook my head.

Annabel opened her wallet anyway, and pressed some money into my hand. "Go on, just get it. You'll regret not buying it. It's so much better than the pink top I was going to lend you."

I stared at the money and then the dress. It really did look good. And I had some savings at home that I could use to pay Annabel back. I grinned. "Okay, thanks! I'll pay you back tomorrow."

By the time we headed back to the fountain to meet the guys, we all had new outfits and accessories for the party. But we hadn't just been shopping. I had put up all our posters for the movie night, while Annabel had managed to get some earrings, a bag and some gift certificates donated for the movie night raffle. Kimmi had talked the art shop owner into giving us some paint for our slushie stand banner. The afternoon had been a great success. The guys could hardly complain about us now.

"So how was the shopping trip?" Liam asked, as we approached.

"What shopping?" Annabel said, managing to sound affronted. She waved a bag at the guys. "These are donations for the movie night raffle."

"And we've got paint for the slushie stand banner," Kimmi said.

"*And* we've put up posters all over the mall," I added.

The guys actually looked impressed.

"How about you?" I asked. "Any luck?"

Liam beamed. "Sloppy Slushie has got a mobile trailer. You know, with a big serving counter at the front – the ones you see at fairs. We can have it for the night. No cost or anything."

"Way to go!" I said excitedly, giving Liam a hug. But I pulled away quickly when I felt his body stiffen.

We stared at each other awkwardly for a moment. It looked like Liam wasn't the hugging type. But I was glad we were friends again.

"So," Liam said eventually. "If you guys are still keen to help out, do you want to meet up next week? Maybe Friday. Give us some last-minute help?"

"Of course," I said. "We'll work on the banner this week. And we can even help set up on Saturday if you want. Before we go to the party."

"Yeah, cool," Jack replied.

"Okay," I said. "Next Friday, then."

We agreed on a time then said good-bye. The guys took off in one direction and we headed in the other.

Mum was meeting us in the parking lot to give us a ride home. I was feeling good again, now that Liam and Jack seemed to have forgiven me for ditching the movie night.

"That actually went pretty well," I said.

"Mmm," Annabel replied, busy on her phone, as usual.

"What's up?" I asked, trying to read over her shoulder.

"Just chatting with Marco," she said.

Kimmi's eyes brightened. "About the party?"

Annabel shook her head. "What are we doing tomorrow?"

"Well," I said, "we could work on the slushie stand banner."

"Then maybe we could go to a movie," Kimmi suggested.

"Or …" said Annabel, grinning. "We could go wakeboarding."

"Wakeboarding?" I said, as we walked outside to the parking lot. "When do we ever do that?"

"Tomorrow afternoon!" she cried. "Because Ryan's dad is taking their speedboat out. And Marco has asked us to come."

Kimmi stopped in her tracks. "You're joking."

Annabel laughed at her. "For real. We're going wakeboarding."

"Marco invited us?" Kimmi's eyes were wide.

"Well, sort of. It was more my idea and Marco made it happen. It'll be fun!"

"It sounds amazing," I said. "Except I can't actually wakeboard. In fact, I'm not even sure what it is."

"It's like waterskiing on a skateboard. But that's not the point!" said Annabel. "Kimmi can hang out with Marco, I can talk to Ryan, and you'll get to meet your new *friend* Saia. He's going too!"

Suddenly it felt like a million butterflies were on the loose in my stomach. "Oh no way, Annabel. You're unbelievable!" I squealed.

Chapter Six

"Just relax, don't force it," Ryan shouted from the back of the speedboat.

I sat in the water, my feet strapped to the wakeboard, clinging to the end of a towrope, getting cold and frustrated. Ryan was being really sweet (and very patient), but there was no chance I could relax.

"Okay, I'll try one more time," I called back. But I was beginning to think I would never get up on the board. All I had managed so far was three face-plants into the water. How embarrassing!

If I'd known it was this hard I never would have agreed to go first. The guys said I'd be able to get up, no problem – and I'd believed them. Big mistake! Now I was just making a fool of myself in front of everyone. I wondered what Saia must be thinking.

"You okay to go?" Ryan asked.

I gave him a wave. *Ready as I'll ever be*, I thought.

I gripped the towrope and pulled my knees to my chest, trying to remember everything I'd been told. Slowly the boat took off ahead of me. I felt the rope pulling on my arms. My legs straightened, but the board stayed behind. My body pitched forward. I was heading for another face-plant, but somehow I managed to lean back far enough for the board to rise to the top of the water, skim across the surface and take my weight. *Finally.* I was up!

I glanced at the boat to see Kimmi throw her arms in the air, cheering. It looked like Annabel was taking a photo. I smiled even wider. I was wakeboarding!

By the time I looked down again, I realized that my board wasn't running directly behind the boat – it had drifted off to the side. I could see the rough water of the boat's wake ahead, but I couldn't steer myself away.

I plowed straight into it. The board flew into the air and I went headfirst the other way. I did a half somersault into the water and felt water gushing up my nose. When I finally got myself the right way up, coughing and spluttering, everyone on the boat was cheering.

"Not bad for your first time," Saia called, as I swam to the back of the boat. I looked at him sheepishly. It was sweet of him to say that, but I knew I was totally useless.

"Yeah, I'm a natural," I said, laughing as I climbed the ladder. "Naturally terrible, that is."

Saia smiled back at me. His smile was even lovelier in real life than it was in his profile pic. "No, you're pretty good. I've seen people take thirty tries to get up. You were up almost straightaway." He put out his hand to help me back onto the boat. I felt goose bumps ripple up my arm as I took his hand. It wasn't the chilly water that was getting to me – it was definitely Saia. He was just as cute as Annabel had promised.

"Nice work, girlfriend," Kimmi called, as I peeled off my wetsuit. I held it out for her to put on, but she shook her head. "Looks way too hard for me."

"Go on," I said. "If I can do it, anyone can."

But Kimmi didn't move. "I'm fine right here, thanks."

Kimmi was sitting between Annabel and Marco, looking very comfortable. Marco had his shirt off and his shades on, leaning back with his hands clasped behind his head, checking out the world with a slight sneer. Yes, he was cool. But didn't he know it!

"Guess it's your turn," I said, handing the wetsuit to Annabel.

She giggled and complained about how cold and clingy the wetsuit was as she wriggled into it. "Here goes nothing," she said, heading for the back of the boat.

"You'll kill it," Ryan said, giving her a wink and a fist bump. Annabel flashed him a great big flirty smile before jumping over the side.

I laughed to myself. Annabel sure knew how to get what she wanted. She and Ryan had only just met, but they sure didn't look like strangers now.

"All set?" Ryan called, as Annabel got into position.

She took hold of the towrope with one hand and gave Ryan the thumbs-up with the other. I held my breath as the boat's engine revved. I knew how hard this was going to be for her. But as the rope tightened, Annabel emerged from the water like some kind of sea nymph – upright, smiling and beautiful. I couldn't believe it. She was up on her first try. Trust Annabel! She was gifted like that – just good at sporty things without even trying.

Ryan punched the air. "Way to go!"

Annabel cruised behind the boat like she'd been doing it all her life. Ryan couldn't take his eyes off her as she soared across the water, her wet hair fluttering in the wind. He was still staring when she finally let go of the towrope, ending her wakeboard session gracefully, rather than spectacularly – like me. Then it was the guys' turn. Marco was first up, handing his shades to Kimmi before getting into the water.

"He's so cute," Kimmi sighed, as the boat took off.

Marco had no trouble getting up. He flew across the water, showing off with twists and turns. Kimmi didn't miss a second of his performance. If she wasn't hooked on Marco before, she certainly was now. But it bothered me that he was so into himself.

Saia wasn't like that at all. He'd only been out a few times on Ryan's boat and didn't have Marco's confidence. He didn't do many tricks and he fell off a couple of times. But even when he did, he kept the same lovely grin on his face. Nothing seemed to annoy him, which made me like him even more. He was still smiling when he climbed back onto the boat. Water droplets were clinging to his lashes, bringing out the deep color of his eyes. He looked so adorable.

"You're pretty good," I said, as he grabbed a towel and dried off.

"Not really," Saia grinned. "Wait till you see this guy."

Ryan got in and showed us what wakeboarding was really about. He did jumps and turns and all sorts of tricks that I wouldn't be able to do on land, let alone on the water. It was totally impressive.

"He's even hotter than I thought," Annabel whispered to me. "I am so going to kiss him next Saturday."

The sun was sinking and the whole harbor was bathed in a glorious golden light as we cruised back towards the marina. On the seat opposite me, Saia had his eyes closed, enjoying the last rays of the late afternoon sun. His skin seemed to be glowing, and I felt a tingle run down my spine just looking at him. Beside me, Kimmi seemed to be in a trance, her eyes on Marco, while Annabel was playing footsie with Ryan.

"Can't wait for the party," said Annabel. "It'll be epic. Shame it's a whole week away."

I smiled to myself. It sounded like Annabel was fishing for an invitation to see Ryan before the party.

"Yeah, it'd be cool to do something before then," he said. "But I've got stuff on tomorrow and then we have practice basically every afternoon next week. We've got a big rugby game next weekend, which we might win, if our coach doesn't kill us first."

Saia groaned. "Oh, man. He's crazy."

"He's like some rabid dog when anyone does anything wrong," said Marco.

Kimmi laughed, way too loudly, and smiled at

Marco. "So, does his rabid-dog style get results?"

Marco shrugged. "Well, we've won every game so far this year. So … I guess."

"Maybe we should come to watch you play next week, then," Kimmi said.

Marco smiled. "Cool. It'll be a close game. Might be a bit ugly, though. Can't promise there won't be any blood."

The guys all nodded.

"What do you like about that game?" Annabel asked. "Seems all you do is smash each other."

"That's why it's fun," said Marco.

The guys all laughed. I guess they had a different idea of fun than us. But I'd noticed they had a different idea about a lot of things. Vacations, for one. Ryan had said his family was going snowboarding in Colorado over the Christmas break. Saia was off to a Pacific island and Marco was visiting family in Italy and planning to do some skiing while he was there. Annabel joined in the ski talk. She'd been to Japan and thought it was totally amazing.

"The snow's unreal, and I love the steam baths," she enthused.

"Oh, yeah," Ryan agreed. "Japan rocks."

"Totes," Kimmi nodded, even though she'd never actually been to Japan.

I stared at my feet, hoping no one would ask what I was doing for vacation. My family was just heading to my grandma's beach house.

It was okay for Annabel. She fitted right in with the Highgrove guys. She lived in a beautiful house right next door to Marco. Her place wasn't as big as his, but it was much, much better than mine. Her family went on cool trips and she always had gorgeous clothes. She was basically like a private school girl who happened to go to Westway. Kimmi was doing a good job of fitting in too, but I felt like a total fraud. I was worried that at any moment, someone was going to realize who I was and throw me overboard.

I looked at Saia as he laughed with his friends about some beach resort I'd never even heard of. I definitely wanted to see him again, and it had been an epic day, but I wondered if Saia and I had enough in common for things to go anywhere.

"Kinda fun hanging out with Highgrove boys, eh?" Annabel said, as we left the marina to find Kimmi's dad who was giving us a ride home. "Ryan is so cool."

"Yeah, I can't wait for the party," said Kimmi. "You know what Marco said?" She paused, twirling her hair in her fingers. "He said I'm too pretty to be at Westway."

"I'm not sure that's a compliment," I scoffed. "He's basically saying that all girls who go to Westway are ugly."

"But he's also saying that Kimmi's pretty – which is true," Annabel said, smiling.

I put my arm around Kimmi. "Well, I guess I can't argue with that."

Kimmi giggled. "Marco is gorgeous. I'm so in lurve!"

"So, you don't think it's all a bit weird, us hanging out with Highgrove guys?" I asked,

"*No*," Annabel said firmly. "Why?"

I shrugged. "Well, what's going to happen at the party? We won't know anyone."

"We'll know the guys. I'm going to be with Ryan, Kimmi's going to be with Marco. And you'll be with Saia."

"Oh, really?" I said, pretending to be surprised.

Kimmi laughed. "Come on. I can tell you like him."

"Well … he does have a pretty cute smile," I said. "But we're so different. I don't know anything about rugby, or skiing or wakeboarding or …"

"No one's going to test you," Annabel interrupted. "Stop panicking for five seconds and chill out. You like Saia and, from the way he's been smiling at you, I can tell he's into you too."

Chapter Seven

By Thursday our plans for Ryan's party seemed to have taken over everything. Annabel, Kimmi and I talked nonstop about what we'd wear, what we'd say and what we'd do.

Annabel and Ryan messaged each other so often they were practically an item. Kimmi had been dreaming about Marco every night, which she took as a sign that things would work out at the party.

Things with Saia were going well, too. Texts were flying back and forth between us, and even though I'd been worried about us not having anything in common, it turned out we did: we both had too much homework and too many annoying teachers. Saia always managed to cheer me up when things at school were bugging me. I could imagine his adorable smile every time he texted me, and I loved the way he always finished his texts with "xx." It was so cute!

But with all the talk of the party, Kimmi and Annabel had completely lost interest in the Wild Club. We hadn't even started working on the banner for the slushie stand. The girls had also gone right off the idea of helping to set up the stand on Saturday afternoon.

"We'll be too busy getting ready for the party," Annabel said, as we headed for our lockers.

"We've got all day to get ready," I said. "I'm sure we'll have time to help set up the stand."

"What about the game?" Kimmi reminded me. "We promised we'd watch the guys play rugby."

I sighed. There seemed to be no point trying to convince them. "Okay, well, even if we can't set up, we should make the banner for the stand. And we still have to go to the Wild Club meeting tomorrow," I insisted. "We promised Jack and Liam we'd be there."

Annabel groaned.

"It's not going to kill you," I said, pausing outside the girls' bathroom. "Look, Bunga needs you." I nodded towards the Wild Club poster, so Annabel and Kimmi would see Bunga's sad eyes staring at them.

"All right, all right," Annabel said. "We'll go to the meeting tomorrow." She turned to the poster of Bunga. "But just for you."

"Bunga says *thank you*," I said in a silly orangutan voice. But as I looked at the poster, I felt guilty all over again that I was going to Ryan's party instead of the movie night. I was well and truly committed to the party now; there was no way I could change my mind. But then I had an idea. Maybe there was still something I could do to help Bunga!

That night, I got through my homework as quickly as possible and then, instead of rereading all the texts I'd had from Saia, like I'd done every other night, I got to work.

By fourth period on Friday, I could feel a knot growing in my stomach as it got closer and closer to lunchtime, when I knew I'd be seeing Liam and Jack. I wondered what everyone in the Wild Club would make of my little project. I'd stayed up late working on it and had only saved it to a USB that morning.

"I still don't know why we're here," Annabel said, as we hovered outside the door. "It's just going to be really awkward. We haven't even done the banner like we said we would."

"Come on," I said. "The guys have probably forgotten all about the banner." I didn't think that was true, but I wasn't going to give Kimmi and Annabel any excuses to get out of the meeting.

"You think?" asked Kimmi hopefully.

"Anyway, I've got something to show Liam and Jack." I waved the USB at them.

"What is it?" Annabel asked nervously. "It's not some random video of us dancing or something is it?"

I shook my head. "Come on, I'll show you." I shoved Annabel and Kimmi in ahead of me. The room was busy with groups of people chatting at full volume, finalizing preparations for the big night.

The guys were huddled together at our usual table, talking.

"Hey, you made it." Liam smiled as we walked in and sat down with them.

"You didn't think we'd come?" I said.

Liam shrugged. "Wasn't sure."

"So, how's the banner going?" Jack asked.

Kimmi glanced at me and scowled. "The paint was still a bit wet," she explained, "so I left it at home. We'll have to bring it to the stand tomorrow."

"Cool," Jack replied. "Can't wait to see it."

"I've got something else to show you," I said, holding up my USB. "I was thinking we should use the fundraiser to educate people about orangutans. So ..." I put the USB into the laptop on the table. Everyone gathered around as I ran the mouse down the files and clicked on *Save the Orangutans*. I could feel Annabel shuffling beside me, getting impatient, but she stopped fidgeting as the music started and footage of some baby orangutans came up on screen.

"So cute," Annabel cooed.

Kimmi started *oooing* and *ahhing* too. "They are so adorable."

I had edited together clips of baby orangutans cuddling each other, clinging to their mother's backs and sucking on babies' bottles. There was some footage of adult orangutans too. My favorite was an old man orangutan brushing his teeth.

"Sweet," said Liam, laughing.

And then came the images of the bulldozers, bringing total destruction to the forest. Kimmi and Annabel stopped giggling.

"What's going on?" Kimmi asked.

"They're clearing the forest for timber and palm oil plantations," I said.

"They can't do that!"

Complete silence fell as some sad footage of starving orangutans followed, showing animals that had been forced out of their forest home by loggers. The film finished with a close-up of a helpless baby orangutan with big, round, sorrowful eyes. The caption read: *We must act now, or orangutans will disappear from the wild by 2023.*

Kimmi wiped a tear from her cheek.

"Wow," Liam said, blinking.

"Powerful stuff," Jack added.

I pulled the USB out of the laptop and handed it to Liam, buzzing from the way everyone had responded to my film. It had really worked. "Hope you can use it somehow tomorrow night," I said. "There might be a laptop you can put it on, or something."

"Thanks," Liam nodded. "It's amazing. I'll make sure it gets used."

I felt a tingle run down my spine as Liam looked at me. He seemed genuinely pleased that I'd gone to so much effort on the presentation.

"It's just a film," I said modestly. "But I wanted to do something to help. I was thinking maybe we could use it to raise awareness outside our school, too. It would be great if we could inspire some other groups to sponsor orangutans."

"That's an epic idea," Liam agreed. "We could set up a website for other schools to access, and link it to one of the orangutan charities."

I couldn't help smiling. It felt great to be in sync with Liam again. I still felt bad about missing the movie night, but I didn't feel so guilty anymore. I knew I'd be involved in the Wild Club's other projects.

By the end of the meeting, Annabel was also excited about staying involved with the club, and Kimmi was determined to make the banner for the slushie stand really special.

"I've got a few ideas," Kimmi said, as we walked off after the meeting. "Do you think we should have a jungle for the background, or should it be a sunset?"

"It doesn't matter what you do," Annabel said, smiling. "It'll be fantastic."

Kimmi shook her head. "I don't want to do the wrong thing."

"How about we help you work on it tomorrow?" I looked at Annabel.

"Sorry," she said. "I'd love to help, but I've got a hair

appointment in the afternoon."

"Oh," I sighed, turning to Kimmi. "Looks like you've just got me for artistic support. I'm useless at art, but I can wash brushes."

Kimmi smiled, putting her arm around me. "Perfect. I'm pretty good at art, but I hate cleaning up. We'll make a great team. We'll get started right after we watch the guys play rugby."

Chapter Eight

"Are these definitely the right guys?" I asked, as we stood on the sidelines of yet another field at Highgrove. We had already spent an hour in the wrong place, watching guys we didn't know play a game that I didn't understand.

"I'm pretty sure I can see Ryan," Annabel said. "On the far side. In the blue top."

"Duh," Kimmi teased. "The whole team is in blue."

"Obviously," Annabel said. "But I'm pretty sure it's him."

I watched as a player in a red jersey charged down one of the Highgrove guys. Another three red guys piled in on top. The ball was totally lost for a while, then it dribbled out the back and the whole process started up again.

"Anyone got any idea what's going on?" I asked.

"One side has to smash the other side out of the way, get the ball to the other end, and stick the ball on the ground."

"And they call this a sport?" Kimmi frowned. And then she squealed. "No way! That's Marco with the ball!"

Next to us, a bunch of girls started cheering as Marco ran. Then they groaned as he was smashed to the ground by a guy twice his size. "Poor Marco," one of them cried.

Kimmi, who had been focused on the game, turned to watch the girls. "Who are they?" she muttered. "And why are they talking about Marco?"

Annabel glanced across at the group. "Probably Fairmount girls," she said. "The one with black hair lives on my street."

"You know her?" Kimmi asked.

Annabel shook her head. "I just recognize her. Can't

say we've ever spoken."

Kimmi seemed completely put out by the girls, who were now whispering to each other and pointing to different players.

"Look how dressed up they are," said Kimmi. "Who are they trying to impress?"

"Totes overdressed," Annabel said.

I nodded, deciding not to mention the fact that we'd spent hours last night texting each other with possible outfits for the rugby game, and that Kimmi was wearing a brand-new top. She clearly wasn't happy about the competition.

I still had my eye on the Fairmount girls when Annabel nudged me. "You might want to pay attention. Your boyfriend's about to score."

"He's not my ..." I began, and then squealed as Saia pounded up the pitch (or was it a field?) with the ball under his arm. "Go, Saia!" I whispered excitedly.

He had one player to get past to reach the goal end. Saia ran straight at him. Then, just as the guy lunged, Saia swerved to the right. The guy missed him completely.

Saia shot to the line and put the ball down right between the goalposts.

The girls beside us screamed and I watched Saia's teammates jump on top of him. I was so proud.

"Saia made a goal!" I shouted.

"It's called a try," Annabel corrected me, suddenly the expert on rugby. "And look! Ryan's about to kick the conversion."

"The what?"

"They get a kick at goal, like a free shot, after they score a try – for extra points," Annabel said.

I watched as Ryan kicked the ball high and long. It sailed right between the posts and over the crossbar. Judging by the squealing that came from the Fairmount girls, it seemed like Ryan had done the right thing. The referee blew his whistle and then the siren went for the end of the game.

The Highgrove guys all jumped on top of each other, celebrating their win.

"Let's go and congratulate the guys," Annabel said, dragging us across the field.

The guys had gathered on the far side for a war cry. I was so excited, I just wanted to give Saia a big hug. But as we moved closer, they left the field and huddled under a tree. Then they sat down while a guy, who I guessed was their rabid-dog coach, started barking at them. It seemed he did that whether they won or lost.

"Oh, man," Annabel complained. "How am I going to give Ryan a kiss with the coach there?"

We hovered for a few minutes, not far from the players, waiting for our chance to talk to the guys, but it seemed they were going to be stuck there forever. Saia was practically facing me, but his head was down.

"Hurry up, crazy coach," Annabel said impatiently. "I've got a hair appointment to get to."

"We should go," I said. "We might get the guys in trouble, hanging around here. Or he might just turn around and shout at us."

Kimmi nodded. "Yeah, we've still got the banner to do, too." She glanced at the Fairmount girls.

"Okay," Annabel sighed. "We can congratulate the guys tonight. Ryan totes deserves a kiss for that!" She waved to him even though he had his back to her.

Kimmi blew a kiss to Marco. He didn't see it either, so I thought it would be safe to blow one to Saia, but just as I did it, he looked up – right at me. He smiled and gave me a wink.

Awkward! I turned away, feeling my cheeks burn. "Saia saw me blowing him a kiss!"

"That's so cute!" Annabel squealed.

"Guess who else was watching?" Kimmi said, nodding to the Fairmount girls, who were looking at us and sniggering.

"Double awkward," I said, grabbing Kimmi's arm and rushing off.

Annabel caught up to us. "I feel sorry for those Fairmount girls," she said. "They can cheer all they want, but the cutest guys on that team are already taken."

I lay on my stomach on Kimmi's kitchen floor, touching up a section of sunset. Kimmi put the finishing touches on a baby orangutan that peered through the palm fronds at the other end of the "Slushies in Paradise" banner.

Finally, she took a deep breath and jumped to her feet. "Finished!"

I put my brush in a jug of water and stood up beside her, admiring the sign. "It's amazing!" It looked like a professional artist had done it. "*You're* amazing!"

"So are you!"

"I didn't do anything. But thank you. Liam is going to be so impressed."

Kimmi frowned.

"Not that it's all about impressing Liam," I added quickly. "But you know how grumpy he got about us going to the party."

"He got grumpy about *you* going to the party," Kimmi said. "With a bunch of cute Highgrove guys. Are you sure there's nothing going on that you haven't told me about?"

I shook my head. "Of course not. Liam and I are friends. He's great. He's passionate about the same things

I am. That's it. And besides, he's in the grade above."

"So you say. But there's no law against dating older guys, you know."

"We're just friends," I said.

Kimmi raised her eyebrows. "So, if he asked you out — to the movies or something — you'd say no?"

"Well, no. I'd say yes," I replied. "Because we're friends." And then I thought about it more. Sure, I'd gone weak at the knees when I first saw him, but then I'd gotten to know him. He really *got* me. He understood what was going on in my head — sometimes better than my friends. I liked hanging out with him in the Wild Club, and of course I'd be happy to see more of him outside school. I liked spending time with him.

"What about if Saia asked you to the movies?" Kimmi asked playfully.

"I think the answer would be yes to that one, too," I said, smiling. A shiver ran down my spine just thinking about Saia's beautiful smile.

"You've got goose bumps!" Kimmi shrieked.

I laughed, trying to stroke down the hairs on my

arms. "That happens every time I think about him. I just melt when he smiles at me."

"So you definitely like him more than Liam?"

I frowned, trying to work it out. "It's totally different. I get a warm, fuzzy, calm feeling when I think of Liam. And with Saia my insides start bouncing up and down. I'm excited to see him tonight, but …"

"You're still worried you're too different?" Kimmi asked.

"What if I get to the party and I really have nothing to say to him?"

Kimmi nudged me. "You know what they say: opposites attract. And if you run out of things to talk about, you can just dance. Or kiss him!"

I laughed. "Is that your plan?"

"Totes," Kimmi said, smiling.

I glanced at the kitchen clock. Annabel would be here any minute to help us with our hair and makeup. She was the closest Kimmi and I were going to get to a stylist. But we were meant to take the banner to school before she got here. We were running really late.

I touched the corner of the banner. It felt almost dry.

"Annabel's going to freak when she finds us still covered in paint," Kimmi said, touching her hair. It was flecked with orange and she had green smudges across her forehead.

"How about you have a shower while I take the banner to school?" I suggested. "Then I'll get changed when I get back."

Kimmi nodded and headed to her room while I carefully rolled up the banner. I couldn't wait to see the guys' expressions when they saw it. But just as I called my mum to ask for a ride, the doorbell rang. I opened the front door to find Annabel in her brand-new white dress, her hair bouncing around her shoulders like she'd just walked off the red carpet.

"Wow," I said. "Ryan is going to pass out when he sees you."

"Thanks. But I'm not sure that's the effect I'm going for." She looked at my shorts and top, frowning.

"I'm not ready to go yet," I said.

"I can see that."

"I'm just taking the banner down to the slushie stand."

"But you don't have time!" Annabel frowned. "They'll just have to live without a banner."

I shook my head. There was no way I was leaving the banner when we'd spent the whole afternoon on it. "I'll be back in a minute, promise."

Annabel sighed. "No, you won't. You'll be ages. And then we'll be late for the party." She looked me up and down. "How about you just put on your dress now, and we'll pick you up from school on our way to the party, It'll be much quicker."

I sighed, realizing I didn't really have a choice.

"Fine, but what about my hair? Don't I need to wash it? Aren't you going to do something with it?"

"It actually looks really nice as it is. You're lucky your hair is just naturally gorgeous."

Annabel sat on the bed as I slipped on my new orange dress. I put on my ballet flats and then turned around to face her. "What do you think?"

"On fire," she said, fluffing up my hair. "You look amazing. You don't need anything, except …" She reached into her clutch and pulled out a lip gloss and some perfume. She sprayed some fragrance at me and then smeared some gloss across my lips. "Perfect." She spun me around to face the mirror. "A bit overdressed for a banner delivery girl, but you're gonna rock the party tonight."

"Thanks!" I grabbed the banner and headed off for the slushie stand.

"I'll message you when we're on our way," Annabel called. "Don't dawdle."

Chapter Nine

A smattering of kids were spread out across the field, marking out their patches of turf with blankets and towels as I picked my way across the grass, clutching the banner. I felt a bit self-conscious arriving in a bright-orange dress when everyone else was in T-shirts, but there was no way I was leaving the banner at Kimmi's after all the work we'd put into it.

As I reached the top of the grassy slope at the edge of the field, I could see the slushie trailer already in position.

I walked over and found Liam on his own in there. He had his back to me and was mixing up a slushie, even though he had no customers at all – probably testing the flavors.

"I'll have seven hundred Borneo Sunsets please," I called, tapping my fingernails on the counter.

He turned, and seemed to do a double take, looking me up and down. "Phoebe, hey! I almost didn't recognize you." He came outside to greet me. "You look like a Borneo Sunset yourself."

I think I blushed like a sunset, too. I wasn't used to getting compliments from Liam, and I guess he wasn't used to seeing me out of school uniform.

"Er, right. I'm not really dressed for a slushie trailer," I said. "I just came to drop off the banner."

His smile fell. "Oh … I thought maybe you'd changed your mind and decided to come and help."

I shook my head, feeling really guilty about going to the party when Liam needed me here. "Are you on your own?"

"Jack's just gone to the bathroom. He'll be back in a sec."

Liam looked at me intently for a moment, as if there

was something important he needed to tell me. Goose bumps sprang up on my arms, and I rubbed them.

"You cold?" Liam said.

"I'll be fine once I'm at Ryan's par—" I stopped mid-sentence as I saw Liam's expression change. He looked hurt. It seemed he really did have a problem with me going to the party.

"So, you want to help me with this banner then?" I said, quickly changing the subject. "We'll surprise Jack with it."

Liam's face brightened and his mood changed completely as we hung the banner from the front of the trailer. It looked even better up than it had on Kimmi's floor. A sunset stretched from one side of the stand to the other, and little orangutans hung from palm fronds on either side of the words *Slushies in Paradise*.

"Unreal," said Liam, nodding approvingly. "You sure you're not a professional artist?"

"Not much to do with me," I said. "Kimmi's the artist. I just did what I was told."

"It *is* you," came a voice from behind.

I turned to see Jack striding towards us.

"Hey, Phoebs, what's it like to have your work in front of the public?"

"Well, only Liam's seen it so far. And now you."

Jack motioned towards the field, where a large crowd had gathered while we were fussing with the banner. "Not the banner!" he said, laughing.

It was only then that I saw what was playing on the big screen. "No way!" I said excitedly. "It's my film."

"Polly said she was going to put it to good use." Liam turned back to me, spread his arms wide and hugged me. "Congratulations! Your debut as a film director."

I felt my body stiffen as he held me, and then the warm fuzzy feeling that I normally got around Liam started going haywire. My heart leapt, and I couldn't tell if it was the excitement of seeing my video or Liam's hug that had caused it. I didn't think he was the hugging type. Where had that come from?

"I'm hardly a film director." I laughed awkwardly. "But I'm glad I could be of some use."

"I'm glad you decided the Wild Club needs you

more than the Highgrove guys," Jack said. "And you're here just in time." He nodded to a gang of kids that were heading up the slope towards the trailer.

"Well, actually, I was just …" I began.

But by then Jack was climbing into the trailer and serving a customer. The line for slushies was growing quickly.

"It'd be great if you could stay," Liam said. "We could really use your help."

I felt a lump in my throat as he looked at me, waiting for a reply. Did Liam want me to stay just because he needed help, or was there more to it? The girls would be on their way to pick me up by now. My phone had already gone off with a bunch of messages, no doubt from Annabel, telling me to hurry up.

"Liam, give me a hand," Jack called from the trailer.

"Coming," Liam called back, his eyes not leaving my face. He looked at me for a moment longer, and then raced off. My insides were in knots as I watched him, wondering what would happen if I stayed. Maybe we would end up on a blanket together under the stars, watching the end of the movie.

I pulled out my phone, checking my messages. There were three from Annabel.

We're coming now. ☺

Almost there. ☺ ☺

Waiting out in front of the school! ☹ ☹ ☹

There was also a message from Saia. My tummy started cramping up as I read it.

Thanks for bringing me good luck at the game today. Can't wait to see you at the party. S xx

I put my phone away and my head in my hands. What was I going to do? Should I stay to help Liam and Jack, or should I go to the party to meet up with Saia?

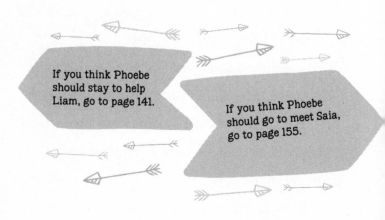

If you think Phoebe should stay to help Liam, go to page 141.

If you think Phoebe should go to meet Saia, go to page 155.

Phoebe GOES TO THE Wild Club *movie night*

Chapter Five

That afternoon, we stood beside the fountain at the shopping mall, where we'd arranged to meet the guys. I still hadn't told my friends what I'd decided to do. I looked at my feet. I didn't want to disappoint them, but the Wild Club was really important to me.

"Listen, I've been thinking," I said. "I've got to go to the movie night."

Annabel's face dropped, like I'd just told her I had an incurable disease. "That is *literally* the worst decision ever."

"You've gotta come to the party," Kimmi begged, pulling on my arm.

I took a deep breath. "How about we *all* go to the movie night? It'll be fun if we do it together," I tried.

Annabel frowned. "That's why we should go to *Ryan's party* together."

"Annabel's right, it won't be the same without you," Kimmi added. "And Marco did make the effort to get us invited. It might seem a bit rude if you don't show up."

I groaned to myself. "I have to help out," I explained. "I've been in the club all year, and I feel bad enough that I didn't go to the last few meetings. I can't just abandon it because I've got a party to go to."

Kimmi looked at me carefully. "Are you sure this isn't about you having a thing for Liam?"

"No!" I insisted. "I told you, we'll never be more than just friends."

"Really?" asked Annabel. "But he's such a hottie. Are you sure you don't like him?"

"Yes!" We'd been in the Wild Club together all year and *nothing* had happened. "I know he's cute, but I'm pretty sure he's not interested."

"Seriously?" Annabel smiled. "So he's free? I mean, you don't mind if I hang out with him a bit?"

"Annabel!" Kimmi and I chorused.

"What about Ryan Baker?" Kimmi asked.

"I still think Ryan's cute. But it's not like he's my boyfriend. I don't even know him, really. Why can't I like two guys?" said Annabel, folding her arms.

"I don't have a problem with you hanging out with Liam," I said to Annabel. "Go right ahead."

"Shh! They're coming!" Kimmi hissed, her eyes darting down the mall.

Liam and Jack were walking towards us. Liam looked his usual relaxed self, probably even *more* chill, now that he was out of uniform. He'd changed into a blue T-shirt that went really well with his eyes. My stomach did a weird little flip.

"Hey there!" I said, a little too brightly. "All ready for work?"

Liam nodded. "Ready as we'll ever be."

Annabel flicked her hair over her shoulder and edged closer to Liam. "We should probably split up if we're going to get everything done. What do you think, Liam?"

"Sure," he shrugged.

Annabel clapped her hands together. "Okay. Kimmi and Phoebs, you can hunt down some paint for the banner. I'll go with the guys to get the slushie machine. Meet you back here in an hour?"

Before I had a chance to work out what was happening, Annabel was leading Liam and Jack up the escalator.

"Wow, that was quick work," I muttered to Kimmi, slightly stunned.

"You know what Annabel's like once she's got her heart set on something," said Kimmi. "But you know, I don't think he's interested in her anyway."

"Oh well, if anyone can talk the slushie store owners into handing over one of their machines, it'll be Annabel," I laughed.

Kimmi hesitated. "Are you sure you're not feeling jealous that Annabel is hanging out with Liam and you're not?"

I sighed and shook my head. "No. I don't think so. It's not like that. It's just …" It was hard to explain. My feelings were all jumbled up. "She wasn't interested in the Wild Club all year, and now she is, but only because of Liam." I took a deep breath and tried to push my feelings aside. "Anyway," I said, grabbing Kimmi's arm. "Come on. Let's go to the art shop."

We wandered off towards the art shop, where Kimmi thought she might be able to get paint for the banner, but I was distracted. My eyes kept darting to the top floor of the mall, hoping to catch sight of the others. I felt a knot forming in my stomach at the thought of Annabel with Liam. He was *my* friend. It didn't seem quite right that she was with him.

"Look there!" Kimmi said suddenly.

My eyes flashed around the top floor, searching for Liam.

"No, there!" Kimmi said, pointing into a jewelry store. She grabbed my hand and pulled me into the middle of the glittering store. Her face lit up with excitement.

Kimmi reached for a bright-pink necklace that was hanging on the wall and held it up. "What do you think? Would this go with the top I'm wearing to the party?"

Before I had a chance to answer, her eyes had darted to another necklace. "Or what about this one?"

I shook my head. "We're really meant to be getting things done for the movie night," I said.

"Oh, yeah," Kimmi sighed, putting the necklace back. Then her face brightened. "Why don't we do both? Let's see if we can get them to donate something for the raffle"

It seemed like a good idea. While Kimmi bought a necklace, I told the store owner all about the movie night and asked if she'd consider donating a raffle prize. She happily handed over a pair of earrings.

Success! Kimmi and I both walked out smiling.

An hour later, back at the fountain, we had a bag full of prizes for the raffle, as well as paint for the Slushies in Paradise banner. We'd put up all of our posters and I was feeling pumped about the movie night again. I couldn't wait to share our success with the others. But as

I watched Annabel coming down the escalator with Liam and Jack, that weird, jumbled feeling came back to me.

Annabel bounced towards us with a grin on her face, like she'd just won first prize in some big competition.

"How'd you do?" I asked.

"Amazing!" Annabel said. "Sloppy Slushie has a mobile trailer that they're going to let us use for the movie night. It's so cute. It's full of slushie machines, with a big window at the front where you serve customers."

"Annabel even convinced them to let us have it for free," said Liam.

Annabel flashed him a bright smile.

"Cool," I said flatly. "That's really great."

I should have been excited about the slushie trailer. It was great news. But I couldn't shake the bad feeling I had. And to make things worse, Annabel kept touching Liam on the arm as she talked. What was that about?

"We scored a cool raffle prize," said Kimmi. She took the earrings out of the bag and showed the others.

Annabel screwed up her nose as she inspected them. "Shame they look kind of tacky."

I could feel my skin prickle. I knew Annabel was right – the earrings were a bit cheap, but she didn't need to say it. "They're actually very expensive," I lied. "And look what else we got."

I pulled out the rest of our donations, doing my best to show the others how hard we'd worked on the fundraiser. I knew I was a being silly, but I just couldn't stop myself. I wanted to impress the guys.

"Good work," Liam said. "Annabel said you'd just be off shopping."

I glared at Annabel.

"Joke!" She laughed, but I didn't see anything funny about it. *She* was the one who loved shopping. And then it hit me. I knew why I was so annoyed with Annabel. She was being fake. She was pretending to be interested in the Wild Club and the movie night, but all she really cared about was getting Liam to like her.

"So, should we meet up again next week, to work out our plans for the slushie stand?" Annabel suggested.

Liam nodded. "How 'bout Monday lunchtime?"

"Sure," said Annabel. "Let's swap numbers, just in

case we need to contact each other about anything. What's your number, Liam?"

It annoyed me that Annabel seemed to be taking over the group, and even though we all swapped numbers, I felt weird that Annabel had Liam's number in her phone. Suddenly everything about her was starting to bug me.

"Liam and Jack are really fun," Annabel said, as we left the guys and wandered off towards the parking lot where Mum was meeting us.

"Shame you're not going to the movie night," I said. "You'd have even more time to hang out with them. I bet the guys are pretty annoyed that you're bailing on the big night."

"Oh, well, about that ..." Annabel gave me a sly grin.

I frowned. "What?"

"Today didn't seem like the right time to tell them," said Annabel. "I didn't want to look like an animal hater."

besides, she was right. I had agreed to help her bake while Mum got the laundry done. "Okay, then. Go get the ingredients out."

Lulu ran out of my bedroom squealing, her tutu bouncing up and down. She'd lasted at ballet lessons for no more than a month, but she really loved that tutu. I changed out of my pajamas and followed her into the kitchen. Lulu was already dragging things out of the pantry. Flour, sugar, breakfast cereal, cake decorations, curry powder – a whole mixture of random ingredients.

I lined up the things that we would need for the brownies and let Lulu measure them into the bowl. She had a look of extreme concentration on her face as she did so, like she was working on a medical breakthrough. She loved to cook, but the problem was that she cooked like she was making mud pies: everything and anything went into the cake mix. One time, she even added peppercorns to a chocolate cake mix when I wasn't looking.

"I'll mix," she declared, when all the ingredients were in the bowl.

I handed her the wooden spoon and stood back. My sister could be very cute when she wasn't whining. Baking was also a good distraction from thinking about Liam and Annabel. Was something really going on with them? They'd almost looked like a couple coming down the escalator at the mall yesterday – so close their hands were almost touching. I should have been happy to see my two friends getting along so well, but for some reason it just didn't feel right. Annabel was a party girl and Liam was a nature boy. They weren't suited at all.

That's when I heard my phone beep.

"Keep stirring," I told Lulu, and headed to my bedroom to find my phone. I had a feeling it would be Kimmi, trying to convince me to go to the party. I fumbled around on my bedside table and checked the message. My heart skipped a beat. It was from Liam.

Hi Phoebe, I have to go to Baitman's Cove today. Do you want to come? My mum is making me help clean up down there. Long story. You don't have to come if you don't want to, but it would be cool if you did. Liam.

I blinked. Liam was asking me to hang out with him

for the day? I felt like the breath had been knocked out of my chest. *Calm down*, I told myself. *He's asking you to pick up trash.* But I was actually excited about it.

Sounds like fun, I replied.

A reply came straight back. *Cool. I'm heading there now. Come down when you can.*

My pulse started racing as I read the message. Liam was leaving for the beach now, but I wasn't anywhere near ready. What was I going to wear? What was the right look for picking up trash at the beach? I could hardly dress up, but I couldn't really dress down either. I flung open my closet and stared at my clothes. I really needed some help on this one. I decided to text Kimmi.

"Pee Pee!" my little sister called.

"Coming," I replied, hastily tapping out a message to Kimmi.

Liam has asked me to meet him at the cove. He's doing some kind of cleanup thing down there and wants me to help.

"Pee Pee!" my little sister yelled again.

I got back to the kitchen just in time. Lulu had

poured the mixture into a baking pan and was about to put it into the oven. I raced to take the pan from her before she spilled it all or burned herself. Mum would freak if she knew I'd let Lulu use the oven alone when I was meant to be looking after her. I slid the pan into the oven just as a message popped up from Kimmi.

Ah-ha! A date! That sounds so cute! ☺

Definitely not a date! I replied, texting with one hand. I slammed the oven door shut and put the timer on with the other. *We're going to be picking up trash! But what do I wear?*

I rinsed the mixing bowl and wiped down the counter, then handed Lulu the ingredients to put away.

Do you have any cute overalls? Kimmi suggested.

Ah, no, I replied. I went back to my bedroom and stared into my closet again.

OK, no idea then, she texted. *Soz, gotta go. But good luck!* ☺

Lulu appeared at the door a moment later. "Whatcha doin'?"

"Thinking," I said absently, pulling out a top and then hanging it up again.

"Where you going?"

"Just going to the cove."

"I'm coming!" Lulu announced, without waiting to be asked.

"Sorry, not this time. I'm doing jobs. It'll be no fun. And you'll get your tutu all dirty."

Lulu frowned and wandered off. I grabbed a T-shirt and a pair of shorts and put them on. I changed another five times before I was finally ready to go to the cove to meet Liam. By then the timer on the oven had gone off. I went to the kitchen and found Mum getting the brownies out of the oven.

"Mum, is it okay if I go down to the cove for a couple of hours?" I asked. "I'm meeting a friend from the Wild Club – we're doing some cleanup project."

"Well, good for you," she said.

"I might take the brownies with me." I took a step towards the counter.

"No!" Lulu shrieked, rushing towards the brownies.

I tried to ease past her. "Lulu, we can make some more later. When I get back."

"No!" She pushed me away, screaming.

Man, she really howled when things weren't going her own way.

"How about you take Lulu to the cove with you," Mum suggested. "Then you can both have the brownies."

"Mu-um, really?"

"Really!" said Lulu.

I looked from Mum to Lulu and then glanced at the clock. If I tried to negotiate my way out of this I might miss Liam altogether. I accepted the deal with a sigh.

A short time later, I was on my way to Baitman's Cove with a basket full of warm brownies and a sister dressed for a ballet concert.

"I'm going to build the biggest sandcastle ever," Lulu said, as we walked down the final set of stairs to the cove. We often came here in the summer. It was still a bit chilly to get in the water just yet, but it was always sandcastle-building weather as far as Lulu was concerned.

"Can you make me a mermaid sandcastle?" she begged.

"We're not building sandcastles," I said. "We're going to be picking up trash."

"I'm going to be picking up shells and treasure!" she replied, skipping down the stairs.

"Okay, whatevs." There was no point arguing with a four year old.

I paused at the bottom of the stairs. From there, I could see the whole cove. There was a small band of volunteers at one end, with trash bags.

I spotted Liam waving at me from the far end of the beach – looking slightly silly. He was wearing a pair of gloves and was armed with long-handled tongs.

"I didn't think you were coming," he said, when we met on the beach.

"Are you kidding? A beach cleanup day? Wouldn't miss it for the world!"

Liam laughed. "Okay, now you're scaring me."

"I'm a ballerina!" Lulu interrupted. "And I've made brownies." Her timing was pretty good because I was sounding a bit weird.

Liam smiled at Lulu. "They smell pretty good."

Lulu nodded and reached for the basket. "Let's eat them."

"Not right now," I said, holding the brownies out of Lulu's reach. "First we're going to help clean up."

She frowned. "First we're going to make a sand mermaid!"

She bolted off across the beach, in the opposite direction from the cleanup volunteers. I watched her go. "I knew this would happen," I mumbled.

"It's cool," Liam said, peeling off his gloves and tossing them in a nearby trash can. "There's hardly any trash left anyway. We should help your sister."

I shrugged. "You think?"

Liam nodded. "Just don't tell my mum. She said if I did four hours down here she'd help me buy a new skateboard. But you know, four hours building sand mermaids is like community service, isn't it?"

"Sure," I laughed. "You actually deserve a medal for hanging out with my sister."

We walked across the sand to join Lulu and got

started on the mermaid. Normally I got bored, making sandcastles with Lulu. But it was a lot more fun with Liam. He put up with all Lulu's silly requests for mermaid scales and special fins. He even laughed when she "accidentally" flung a whole handful of sand on his head.

"Sisters, eh?" he laughed, shaking the sand out of his floppy blond hair. "Mine are even bossier."

As Lulu went off to find shells to decorate the mermaid, Liam told me more about his family. His sisters sounded funny, and his parents seemed really cool. They studied coral reefs, and his whole family were vegetarians.

"I'm trying to be a vegetarian, too," I told Liam. "But Mum keeps sneaking meat into my meals, thinking I won't notice. I wish I had your parents."

"No you don't, they're completely nuts," said Liam. "I think it's because they spend all their time with their heads underwater, looking at coral. All that water has to do something to your brain."

"Maybe it's good for you," I suggested, starting to dig a tunnel underneath the mermaid.

"Let's hope you're right because I spend almost every vacation with my head underwater, too. We go scuba diving a lot."

"Sounds amazing. What's the best thing you've seen diving?"

"Sharks are cool," said Liam thoughtfully. "I can identify over a hundred different species."

I shivered. "You swim with sharks?"

Liam nodded, tunneling under the mermaid from the other side. "Sometimes. Not great whites, if I can avoid them."

"Sounds like you go on exciting trips."

Liam nodded. "Always."

As Liam told me about a trip to a turtle nesting site on the Great Barrier Reef, I pushed my hand into the tunnel under the mermaid to collect another handful of sand and touched something. When it wriggled, I realized it was Liam's fingers.

"Oh, sorry," I said.

As I jerked my hand away, my whole arm tingled. I looked at Liam. His eyes had gone all intense, like he was shocked or something. He stared at me for a moment without saying anything, then looked away. He flicked the hair from his face and smoothed out the mermaid's tail.

And that's when I noticed the color of his eyes. Like, really noticed them. I'd always known they were blue, but I saw for the first time that they were exactly the same as the aquamarine in my mum's engagement ring – a vibrant blue, like they'd been chipped from a precious stone. They were gorgeous. And they matched the rest of him perfectly. Liam was clever, interesting and caring – a totally gorgeous person all around. I realized that even though I liked him as a friend, there might be more to it.

"That is the best mermaid ever," Lulu said, returning with her shell collection and interrupting my thoughts. She carefully placed her decorations around the mermaid's waist and then clapped her hands. "Now we can have the brownies!"

"Okay," I said, wiping my sandy hands on my top. I unwrapped the brownies, noticing that my hands were trembling slightly after our unexpected encounter in the mermaid tunnel. I just hoped Liam didn't notice.

"Mmm," Lulu purred, closing her eyes and sniffing.

The brownies were still warm and they smelled heavenly – although there was something a bit different about the smell that I couldn't quite put my finger on. Lulu leaned across me to snatch one, but I offered them to Liam first.

"*Wow*, they look good," he said, taking a brownie and putting the whole thing in his mouth.

I smiled for a moment, proud that Liam was enjoying one of my homemade brownies, but I knew something was wrong as soon as I heard a crunch. Liam's face twisted as he swallowed. He jumped to his feet, ran towards the end of the cove and flung himself behind a boulder. I turned to Lulu. By that stage she had a mouthful of brownie, too. A moment later she showered me with chewed-up brown mush. "Blahhhh!"

"Lulu!" I shrieked, flicking bits of saliva and brownie off my face. "What did you put in those brownies?"

"Those chocolate chips taste yucky!" she cried, still

spitting out bits of brownie onto the sand.

"What do you mean, chocolate chips? We didn't use chocolate chips. We don't even *have* chocolate chips!"

Lulu nodded. "We do. In the blue container."

I shook my head. Why did I never learn? "Those aren't chocolate chips, they're dog biscuits!"

I turned to check on Liam. He was hunched over behind the rocks. It looked like he was vomiting. Lulu had probably poisoned him!

Chapter Seven

"Wait here!" I shouted at Lulu as I rushed off to see if Liam was okay.

"What about the brownies?" Lulu asked.

"Give them to the seagulls," I called over my shoulder. At least the birds would appreciate them.

Liam was at least standing upright by the time I reached him. He looked awful though, pale and queasy.

"You all right?" I asked.

Liam wiped his mouth. "Yeah, think so. Sorry, that was gross. Guess I had an allergic reaction to the brownies. I don't feel too good."

"Oh, that's bad luck." I couldn't admit that I'd fed

him dog biscuits. He was a vegetarian! "Can I get you a drink? I've brought some juice."

A flash of panic swept across Liam's face. "No, no, no. I'm fine. Honestly."

He backed away from me, still looking nervous. It was understandable that he didn't want to share my juice after I'd nearly killed him with the brownies.

"I think I might go home," he said. "Not feeling too good at all. I mean, the brownies were amazing and everything. I've just got a really sensitive stomach."

"I could walk you home if you like. Make sure you're okay," I said, stepping towards him. He was so pale.

He opened his mouth to reply, but was interrupted by my sister's screaming.

"Pee Pee!"

I glanced at Liam. He was still looking terrible, but now he was trying to stifle a smirk. "Think your sister needs the bathroom."

I rolled my eyes. "Yeah, guess so. Can't take her anywhere," I joked. There was no way I was going to admit that *Pee Pee* was my nickname. I turned to my sister, who was being bombed by squawking seagulls. It looked like they'd found the brownies and were about to carry Lulu off, too.

"Pee Pee!" she shrieked, over the top of the birds.

"You'd better go," Liam said. "I'm going to head off." He paused for a moment, holding his stomach. "I'll see you at school."

"Yeah, sure," I said. "Thanks for inviting me. It's been fun."

"No probs." He grimaced. He didn't look like he was having fun at all.

I hesitated for a moment and then ran off to save my sister. When I reached Lulu, I looked over my shoulder and saw Liam on the stairs. I waved to him, but he didn't see me. I turned to Lulu.

She was clutching a handful of brownies. Her eyes were as wide as Frisbees and her body was frozen in panic. "I hate seagulls," she whimpered.

I pried the brownies out of her hand and threw them towards the sea. The birds took off after them as I dragged Lulu in the opposite direction. As we trudged off, Lulu sniveled. "I don't like this beach."

"I told you it would be no fun," I grumbled.

I took out my phone and sent a text to Liam wishing him a speedy recovery.

Then I texted Kimmi.

Disaster at Baitman's Cove! Just poisoned Liam with dog biscuits.

Kimmi got straight back to me. *Silly question. But HOW?*

I left my sister in charge of the brownies! ☹ I replied, sighing.

Too funny! Kimmi replied. *I might try that one on my brother! Meet you at the playground in ten minutes?*

"Sup!" Kimmi called, as she walked across the playground towards us with a great big smile on her face. Kimmi's smile was usually infectious, but today it wasn't working on me at all. I pushed Lulu higher on the swing, the events at the beach still swishing around in my mind.

"I'm such a loser," I groaned.

Kimmi laughed. "You fed Liam dog biscuits. He'll forgive you. You're friends, right?"

I took a deep breath, giving Lulu another push. I shrugged.

"What?" Kimmi asked. "You're not friends anymore?"

I sighed. "I'm not sure. I think maybe you were right yesterday."

Kimmi raised her eyebrows. "Oh?"

"I might have a *thing* for Liam. Just a small thing. Or maybe a medium-sized one."

Kimmi clapped her hands together. "I knew it!"

I shook my head. "And now I've tried to poison him. You should have seen the look on his face as he ran off. I'm not even sure I'll be able to go to the Wild Club on Monday. I feel so stupid."

Kimmi squeezed my arm. "Don't be silly. It wasn't even your fault. There's nothing to feel stupid about."

"It's not just the poison brownies. What about Annabel? You saw the way she was touching his arm every five seconds at the mall."

"I guess." Kimmi thought for a moment and then shook her head. "But she'll understand if you explain."

I sighed. "I suppose." But I didn't feel any better.

"A big push!" Lulu shouted as her swing slowed, almost stopping.

Kimmi nudged me aside and took over, sending Lulu high into the air.

"Liam invited *you* to the cove, didn't he?" Kimmi said.

"To pick up trash," I grumbled. "He didn't invite me to the movies or anything."

"*Still*, he obviously likes you. You've probably been too wrapped up in orangutans to notice."

I sniffed. "I think I might have noticed if a guy had a crush on me."

As the swing slowed, Lulu jumped off and ran over to the slide.

"Yeah, so you keep saying," said Kimmi, sitting down on the empty swing. "I think you're using that as an excuse not to go after Liam, when anyone can see how much you like each other. Sometimes you just have to show a guy how you feel."

"Is that what you're going to do at the party? Show Marco how you feel?"

Kimmi laughed. "I think I've blown enough kisses at Marco to show him how I feel. Just waiting for him to blow one back, now."

"It'll happen at the party," I smiled.

"Hope so." Kimmi wrinkled her nose, looking uncertain, then stretched out her legs to get her swing going. "Come on, enough about boys. I bet I can swing higher than you."

I sat on the other swing, and together we flew back and forth. We soared so high, I felt like my feet were almost touching the clouds. With each upward swing, my worries about Liam slipped off my shoulders. I swung high, then jumped off and landed in the grass. I rolled over on my back and looked up at the clouds floating across the sky.

Kimmi landed beside me. Then Lulu was running

towards us, her mud-stained tutu bouncing around her middle, looking as elegant as a baby hippo. She did a flying leap and landed on top of me.

"Pee Pee!" she laughed. She held out a scrunched-up little fist. "I've got something for you." Slowly, she uncurled her hand.

I stared at a crumpled green thing on her palm.

"A four-leaf clover," she said. "I found it for you."

I didn't hold out much hope for a change in my luck. But as we were walking home, a message from Liam appeared on my phone. He'd finally replied to my text.

"What's it say?" Kimmi asked, looking over my shoulder.

Feeling OK now, the message read. It came with a picture of a new skateboard. *Guess where I'll be this afternoon?*

I looked at the picture for a moment and then handed the phone to Kimmi. Her face broke into a smile.

"Are you thinking what I'm thinking?" she asked.

I was thinking a lot of things, but mainly I was relieved. Liam had survived the dog biscuit brownies and was still talking to me – which was way more than I had expected. "That depends," I said. "Are you thinking it's weird how guys get so excited about a short plank of wood?"

Kimmi slapped me playfully on the arm. "I'm thinking we should go to the skate park."

"Are you serious? You want to just randomly turn up?"

Kimmi nodded. "I'd say that text was basically an invitation to do just that."

I reread the text. I couldn't see an invitation in there at all. "I think he's just letting me know that he's alive."

Kimmi shrugged. "The skate park is almost on the way back to your house, so we could swing by and check it out."

I gave it some thought. "Couldn't hurt, I guess."

I grabbed Lulu's hand and we walked off towards the skate park. I really didn't want to seem like a skater groupie, but Liam and I were friends. Surely it would be okay to take a look, just to make sure he really was all right after the brownies. I was pretty sure he hadn't invited me to the skate park, but it would be cool to see him on his new board. I made sure I had my lucky four-leaf clover in my pocket, hoping it would work some more magic.

Kimmi, Lulu and I paused behind a tree not far from the skate park to check out the situation. The ramps were busy and the guys were wearing helmets, so it was hard to spot Liam. I thought I'd know him straightaway, but there were a lot of guys who looked just like him. The one that stood out was a tall guy, a bit on the lanky side.

"That's Jack, isn't it? With the black helmet. He's just about to go down the ramp."

Kimmi peered at the guy. "I think it is. Guess he's down here with Liam."

"We should go over and say hey."

"Yeah," Kimmi said, but she didn't move. She just stood watching Jack negotiate the ramp. He was pretty unreal.

"Kimmi?" I said, nudging her. "Are you checking out Jack?"

"I might be," Kimmi said coyly.

I laughed. "I thought you only had eyes for Marco."

She sighed. "I do, but I wonder if he's ever going to see *me*."

"Of course he will."

Kimmi paused. "But what if he's not into me at all?"

Now it was my turn to offer support. "Oh, come on. Everything will work out at the party. You'll see. I bet you two are together by the end of the night."

The smile returned to Kimmi's face. "You're right," she giggled. "How could he resist me?"

"Let's go ask Jack where Liam is hiding," I said, taking Lulu by the hand. But I'd only taken a few steps when I froze, then dived back behind the tree, dragging Lulu with me.

"What's going on?" Kimmi asked.

I nodded to the far side of the skate park. I'd just spotted a guy with his helmet under his arm and hair flopping into his eyes. It was definitely Liam. But it was the girl who was with him that was giving me heart palpitations. She flicked her blond hair over her shoulder as she chatted to Liam. It was painful to watch, but I couldn't take my eyes off them.

"It's Annabel," Kimmi gasped.

Just as she said that, Lulu jumped out from behind the tree. "Annabel!" she shouted. Annabel spent a lot of time at our house and Lulu adored her.

I grabbed my little sister and jerked her back behind the tree. "Shh," I hissed. "It's like hide-and-seek and Annabel's it. We can't let her know we're here."

We edged back the way we'd come, then raced around the corner so there was no chance we'd get caught spying on them. When we stopped, I could feel my heart thumping. There was a sick feeling rising in my stomach.

"This is worse than I thought," Kimmi puffed. "Annabel must really like Liam."

I winced. A sharp pain was developing in my chest. "Well, I did tell her we were just friends."

Kimmi looked down, distracted by something on her phone. Then her face froze. "Oh no," she frowned. "Do you want to see this?"

I shook my head, but looked anyway. My heart sank as I saw Annabel's latest post. It was a picture of her and Liam at the skate park. Annabel was wearing Liam's helmet. The post read: *How do I look?*

It had been up only a few minutes and it already had ten "likes" and three comments – everyone telling Annabel how cute she looked and asking about Liam.

That was when I knew for sure: I had no chance with him at all. If Liam had to choose between Annabel and me, he'd definitely choose her. She was confident and pretty. Guys just loved her.

All I had to look forward to was a status update from Annabel announcing that she and Liam were "in a relationship." I wondered if that would happen before the end of the weekend.

Chapter Eight

On Monday morning, I took my seat on the bus next to Annabel and Kimmi, still not feeling great after possibly the worst weekend ever.

"Looks like you had a good weekend," I said to Annabel, trying to manage a smile. I'm not sure why I mentioned it because I didn't want to hear about Annabel's weekend. If she went on about how much fun she'd had with Liam, I wasn't sure how I'd handle it.

"Not too bad," she said mysteriously, giving us a slight smile.

"Cute pic of you in Liam's helmet," said Kimmi. "What's going on?"

Annabel shrugged. "He's like a cryptic crossword – so hard to work out. But I think I'm getting it. I'm hoping to unlock his secrets at the Wild Club meeting at lunchtime."

"Yeah, should be a great chance," I muttered.

"Something wrong?" Annabel asked. "You don't mind me hanging out with Liam, do you? You said you were just friends."

I laughed. "Me? Mind? Of course I don't mind."

I could see Kimmi was about to say something, but she closed her mouth when I glared at her. I didn't want Annabel to know what was really going on in my head. If Liam and Annabel were into each other, I'd deal with it. I'd just go back to being friends with Liam. I didn't want to fight with Annabel over a guy.

Annabel looked out the window dreamily. "Liam's so gorgeous. You should have seen him at the skate park."

"Wish I'd been there," I said, relieved that Annabel was too caught up in Liam to notice how my voice wobbled. I took a deep breath, determined to be a good friend. "So, what did you find out about him?"

Annabel shrugged. "He doesn't talk much, really. More of an action man."

I nodded. But I was surprised to hear that Liam was quiet. He was always chatty with me in the Wild Club and he'd had loads to say when we were building the mermaid together. Once I started thinking about that, all I could feel was the electric current that had run through my body when our fingers touched in the tunnel. I looked away from Annabel in case she could tell what I was thinking. Why had it taken me so long to work out that I liked Liam?

"Do you think we make a good couple?" Annabel asked.

"Aren't you forgetting about someone?" Kimmi interrupted before I had a chance to answer.

Annabel raised her eyebrows.

"A certain guy called Ryan Baker?" Kimmi said. "We're going to his party on Saturday, remember?"

Annabel giggled. "Of course I haven't forgotten about Ryan. But he's at Highgrove and Liam's at Westway. And I get to see Liam at lunchtime to talk about the slushie stand. I'm getting goose bumps just thinking about it. Weird, huh?"

"Yeah," I said. But I knew just how she felt because I was feeling exactly the same way. The hairs on my neck stood on end at the thought of meeting up with Liam. "When are you going to tell him you're not going to the movie night?" I couldn't stop myself from asking.

Annabel grimaced, looking uncomfortable. "Not today. Do you mind not saying anything to them yet? I don't want Liam to think I'm an airhead who only cares about parties."

I glanced across at Kimmi. She was shaking her head at me.

"Sure." I smiled, ignoring Kimmi. But a little bit of me was dying inside. Now I wasn't just standing aside to let Liam and Annabel get to know each other, I was actually agreeing to deceive Liam, so he would like Annabel more.

But what else could I do? I had to stick by my friend. I'd told her Liam and I were just friends. It was too late to change my tune now.

I gazed out the window, trying to work things out in my mind. At least I'd have Liam to myself at the movie night. But I wondered how I'd survive until then. Watching Annabel flirt with him was going to drive me crazy.

Beside me, Annabel was telling Kimmi about how she was getting into skating now. She had some money saved, and was going to buy a board. Liam was going to teach her how to ride it.

I sighed to myself. There was no way I'd be able to endure this all week.

"All set to meet the guys?" Annabel asked, as the bell rang for lunchtime. "I can't wait to tell them my ideas for the slushie stand."

"I think we should tell them that we're not going to the movie night," Kimmi said. "It's not fair to spring it on them at the last minute. They'll be expecting us to help."

Annabel stopped in her tracks. "Please," she said, grabbing Kimmi by the arm. "We'll tell them later. Soon, I promise. Just not today."

Kimmi rolled her eyes. "Fine. But Liam's going to find out sooner or later, and he's going to be more annoyed if it's later."

Annabel didn't seem to hear. She was striding ahead towards the science building where the meeting was being held. I knew I couldn't follow. There was no way I could sit in a room with Annabel and Liam.

"Oh no!" I cried suddenly. Kimmi and Annabel both turned to look at me. "I've just remembered I've got a debate team meeting today," I said, slapping my forehead.

"But what about our Wild Club meeting?" Kimmi asked.

I shook my head. "I can't make it after all." I turned and started running in the opposite direction. "Say sorry to Liam and Jack for me!"

"How was your meeting?" I asked, when I saw Annabel and Kimmi at the lockers after lunch. "Learn anything interesting about Liam?"

Annabel frowned. "I learned not to ask Liam about endangered animals. Turns out he isn't so quiet when it comes to that topic."

I smiled to myself. I was sorry I'd missed it – I loved hearing Liam talk about wildlife. Trying not to dwell on that, I asked, "Anything else?"

"I found out that Jack's really good at painting," Kimmi said, blushing slightly as she mentioned Jack's name. "We're working on the banner for the slushie stand together. He's really talented."

Kimmi banged her locker shut and checked her phone. I couldn't help noticing that she was reading a message from Jack.

"Is there another Wild Club romance blossoming?" I asked, looking at Kimmi.

She pressed her phone to her chest. "Wouldn't you like to know."

"Yes, I *would*," I said, pretending to be indignant.

"You'll have to come to the next meeting and find out for yourself," she said. "We're seeing the guys again on Wednesday."

I grabbed my books. "Okay, sounds good."

But in the end I didn't go. That week at school was the worst. Annabel talked about Liam so much on Monday and Tuesday that by the time Wednesday came around I couldn't bear the idea of going along and watching her flirt with him. Just as the girls were headed off to the meeting, I made up another debate emergency and rushed off in the other direction. Then on Friday, when everyone was meeting up again, I pretended to be sick and spent lunchtime in the bathroom.

It was awful. I really wanted to help out with the stand, but I didn't want to be around when Annabel was making eyes at Liam. I decided it was best to help Kimmi and Annabel out with the things they were organizing for the slushie stand, and not see Liam at all.

The most important thing was that I would be there on the night to help out with the stand. Kimmi and Annabel would be at the party, and I would be able to hang out with Liam, without Annabel twirling her hair and getting in the way. Sure, Liam and I could only be friends, but that was better than nothing. I wished I'd never talked Annabel into joining the Wild Club in the first place.

"You feeling okay now?" Kimmi asked, as we headed off to French after I'd spent lunchtime in the bathroom.

"Much better, thanks. Did I miss anything important in the meeting?" I wasn't sure I really wanted to know, but I had to ask.

"Jack drew me the cutest little monkey. Look how intricate it is." She handed me a picture of an emperor tamarin.

"It's beautiful," I said, handing back the drawing. "But I meant, did I miss any stuff I need to know for tomorrow night?"

"It's all pretty organized," Annabel said. "But there'll be a bit to set up, so we'll need to get there early tomorrow."

"*We?*" I asked. "I thought you were going to Ryan's party?"

Kimmi and Annabel glanced at each other. "Totes," Annabel said. "But we'll give you a hand to set up first. There'll be a lot to do."

It wasn't really what I wanted to hear. I wanted them to go to the party and have fun with Marco and Ryan. I didn't need them at the slushie stand. But Annabel was adamant. She and Kimmi would help set up.

"So, how are things going with Liam?" I asked Annabel, torturing myself some more on the bus trip home.

"Oh, so great," Annabel replied. "I feel like we've known each other forever. We've just *clicked* this week. He's so cute and clever. I can't wait until we're really going out. I'm hoping he'll ask me tomorrow." She gave me a smile that almost made me sick. Just listening to her talk about Liam like that was enough to turn my stomach.

"Of course, it's going to be tricky with you two in different grades," I said. "That never works out."

"There's no law against it, you know," Annabel replied calmly.

"Yeah, obviously," I said. "But it's kind of an unwritten code. You can't break those."

"Is everything okay?" Annabel asked. "You kind of seem in a bad mood."

"Fine," I replied, feeling guilty. I knew I was being nasty, but I couldn't help myself – it made me feel a bit better.

"I know it's hard when your friends get boyfriends, you kind of feel left out," Annabel said.

Kimmi put her arm around me. "You're actually looking a bit pale. Sure you're okay?"

"It's fine. I'm fine. I'm not like you two, anyway. I don't *need* a boyfriend." I didn't want anyone right now. I just wanted to run away to a jungle and hang in a tree with an orangutan.

"We're just trying to help," Kimmi sighed, taking her arm away.

"Yeah, I know. Sorry." I felt bad for being mean. Again. It wasn't Annabel's fault that Liam liked her. And Kimmi was just being sweet. I knew they were just trying to help, but they were making things worse.

I was still feeling annoyed the next day. The movie night was just a few hours away and I felt uneasy about going. Seeing as Annabel and Kimmi were going to help set up before going to the party, the plan was to meet at Kimmi's place and go to the movie night together from there.

I took a deep breath. I just had to suck it up and get used to things. Annabel and Liam were almost an item. I couldn't hide from it forever.

I had just pulled on some clothes, ready to head to Kimmi's, when my phone buzzed with a text. I was running late, so I figured it would be Annabel telling me to hurry up. But the message was from Liam.

Are you still coming to the movie night?

It seemed a strange question, but I hadn't been to the meetings all week, so maybe he'd guessed something was wrong.

Yes!! Just getting ready to leave now, I replied, pushing away any ideas about not going until later. The guys would need my help.

A text pinged back almost immediately. *Where have u been all week?*

I felt a little bit excited that Liam had actually noticed that I'd been missing.

Soz, debate commitments. Couldn't get out of them.

Nothing to do with your boyfriend commitments? he replied.

My heart skipped a beat. Boyfriend? Where did he get the idea that I had a boyfriend?

No boyfriend commitments. U know me. I only have eyes for Bunga the orangutan.

I stared at the screen for a minute, waiting for a reply. When it finally came, I almost dropped my phone.

Annabel said u had a boyfriend.

I felt my stomach churn. What was going on? Surely

Annabel hadn't told Liam I had a boyfriend. He must have misunderstood.

What?? I dashed back.

She said u had a boyfriend at Highgrove. That's y ur too busy for the Wild Club.

I read the message again, then again and again. But there seemed only one way to interpret it. Annabel had lied. But why?

I definitely don't have a boyfriend, I replied. *C u tonight. Never too busy for Wild Club!*

I flopped onto my bed, almost too stunned to move. Liam's texts kept going around and around in my head.

I picked up my phone to text Annabel. I had to understand why she'd lied. Then I changed my mind, packed up my bag and headed to Kimmi's. I couldn't work this out by text. I had to talk to Annabel in person.

Chapter Nine

I was feeling totally stressed out as I buzzed Kimmi's front doorbell. I had no idea how I was going to handle things with Annabel. I couldn't just walk in and accuse her of lying. There was no way we'd stay friends after that. On the other hand, there was no way I *could* be her friend if she had lied to Liam. I just hoped it was all some silly misunderstanding.

"Phoebe!" Kimmi smiled as she opened the door. "You look so cute. Love that necklace on you."

I gave her a hug. She smelled like a bunch of fresh flowers and looked just as pretty. "I don't look nearly as cute as you. Love those shorts. Did you get them today?"

Kimmi nodded. "I'm so excited about tonight." She did a little shoulder shuffle as we walked towards her room, to prove the point. "Do you think Jack will like the outfit?"

I frowned. "You mean Marco?"

She hesitated for a moment. "Well, we'll be at the movie night for a while."

"Sure," I said. "But then you're going to the party, right? To see Marco."

Kimmi nodded. "Mmm."

"You *have* told Liam and Jack you're going to the party, haven't you?"

Kimmi shook her head. "Not yet."

"What?"

"We didn't want to disappoint them," Kimmi said, looking uncomfortable.

I couldn't work out what was going on with Kimmi, but there was something I needed to discuss with her before Annabel appeared.

"Kimmi!" came a voice from the bedroom. "Is that Phoebs? We have to get going."

I froze at the sound of Annabel's voice, grabbed Kimmi by the hand, and dragged her off to the kitchen. "I have to tell you something," I whispered urgently. I knew I didn't have much time.

"What?" Kimmi asked, leaning towards me with a concerned look on her face.

"I had a text," I whispered. "From Liam."

I pulled out my phone and showed her the exchange. Kimmi read through it, her eyes getting wider. Then she gasped.

"Why would Annabel say I had a boyfriend?" I asked. "Or that I was too busy for the Wild Club?"

Kimmi reread the text, shaking her head. "I have no idea. You'll have to ask her."

"Kimmi! Where are you?" Annabel called.

"No more secrets," Kimmi whispered. "You need to find out what's going on."

I nodded. "Okay."

Annabel appeared at the kitchen door. She stiffened for a moment when she saw me. "What are you guys doing in here?"

"Just grabbing a drink," I replied, helping myself to a glass and grabbing some water from the fridge. I glugged it down.

"Has Kimmi told you the news?"

My heart thumped as I wondered what she was going to tell me. "What news?"

"We're coming to the movie night!"

"Yeah, I know," I said, still confused. "To set up."

"No, we're staying to help on the stand. We decided not to go to the party after all. We're going to stay and hang out with you all night!"

I glanced at Kimmi. No wonder she'd been so vague about going to the party.

"Oh, great," I said, trying desperately to sound enthusiastic. It wasn't easy with my insides twisting. This was a disaster. All week I'd been thinking that I couldn't bear to see Annabel flirting with Liam, and now it was going to happen in front of me all night.

But Liam's text did make me think that he wanted me to be there tonight. Was he really worried that I had a boyfriend? Or did he just want me there as a friend?

And if that was true, maybe we could just go back to being friends, and things could be like they were before they got all tangled up. This could be the chance for us to straighten everything out. We could all have a fun night together, working at the slushie stand.

"Love the way you've done your hair, by the way," Annabel said.

"Thanks." I don't know what I'd expected, but I guess I didn't think Annabel would be so nice. I'd spent ages on my hair, making it right for tonight. But was Annabel being sweet, or was she laying on the compliments because she felt guilty about lying to Liam?

Annabel grabbed my hand and led me through to Kimmi's room. "I brought that top I said you could borrow." She pointed to a pink top on the bed. "And these wedges go so well with it, you could wear them too. I know we're not going to the party, but it will be fun to dress up anyway."

I looked at the top and then stared at the wedges. They were brand-new – hardly the thing to wear to slop around in slushie spillage.

"But you haven't even worn them," I said, feeling torn. They were gorgeous.

Annabel pushed them into my hands. "That's okay. They're a bit tight for me, but they'll look great on you."

Annabel was being her generous self. I kicked off my old flats and bent down to put on the wedges, hoping they'd fit. They were perfect. "Are you sure I can wear them at the slushie stand? They might get a bit dirty."

Annabel nodded enthusiastically and threw me her top. "Try that on, too."

I hesitated for a moment, running my fingers over the texture of the fabric. It felt like real silk. Probably not the best choice for a slushie stand, either. But it was so gorgeous that I pulled off my own shirt and slipped on Annabel's.

"What d'you think?" I asked, twirling around in front of the girls.

"Perfect!" Annabel clapped, giving me a big smile. "You have to wear it."

I studied myself in the mirror. I still didn't look as

good as Kimmi or Annabel, but I looked so much better than I had when I first arrived.

"Sure you don't mind me wearing your stuff?" I asked Annabel. "I'm going to be pouring slushies."

"Just wear it," she insisted. "It looks great on you."

I glanced at Kimmi, who had a serious expression on her face. "I think you've got something to ask Annabel, haven't you, Phoebs?"

I gulped. I didn't want to argue with Annabel. Now definitely wasn't the time to be accusing her of lying. Not when we were going to spend the whole night together working on the slushie stand.

"I was?" I said, pretending I'd forgotten. I gave Kimmi a pleading look.

But Kimmi wasn't going to let me off that easily. "About Liam," she said. "You've got something to ask Annabel about Liam."

My heart almost stopped beating as Annabel turned to look at me.

"What about Liam?" she asked.

My eyes darted from Kimmi to Annabel, wondering

what to say. Did I really want to ruin everything by asking her if she'd lied to Liam? Or should I keep the peace and pretend nothing was wrong?

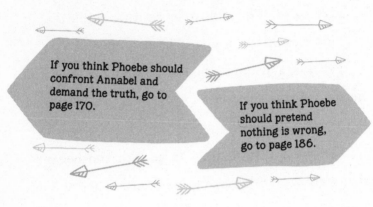

If you think Phoebe should confront Annabel and demand the truth, go to page 170.

If you think Phoebe should pretend nothing is wrong, go to page 186.

Phoebe STAYS TO help Liam

Chapter Ten

I watched the line at the slushie trailer growing longer, a sense of panic rising inside me. Then I did the only thing that felt right. I pulled out my phone to text Saia.

Glad you won today. Really, really sorry, but I can't make the party. Family emergency. Have fun tonight. P xx

I pressed the send button. It felt awful to let Saia down. He might not ever talk to me again after this, but I knew that I had to stay at the slushie stand and help Jack and Liam.

I felt a twinge of jealousy at the idea of Saia being at the party with a whole bunch of private school girls. If they were anything like those Fairmount girls I'd seen at the rugby game, well … I didn't even want to think about it. But I'd made my decision and I knew this was the right place for me to be. Now I had to face my biggest challenge: telling Kimmi and Annabel.

Jack and Liam have me tied to the slushie trailer. Can't escape. So sorry! Have fun at the party. Told Saia it's a family emergency. Good luck! P xxx PS Don't come looking for me or you might get roped in too.

A reply came straight back from Annabel: *Stop being Miss Student-Rep Wild-Club girl, and get your butt up here. We're out in front. Waiting!*

Sorry. No can do, I texted back. *My heart belongs to the orangutans. And my film's up on the big screen! P xxx*

Kimmi replied to that. *Congrats! We're going to miss you ☹☹☹ But we'll try to have fun without you. XXXXXXOOOOO ☺☺☺*

I put my phone back in my bag and headed off to help the guys.

Liam stared at me anxiously as I climbed into the trailer.

"Anyone got an apron?" I asked, smiling.

A massive, beautiful grin spread across Liam's face. And I got that lovely fuzzy feeling that I was used to. Yes, I'd definitely made the right choice. This was where I belonged.

Jack turned around from the slushie machine and stared at my dress. "Nice outfit for pouring slushies."

"Well, I wasn't exactly planning to stay."

"Glad you changed your mind," Liam said, holding out a dish towel. "D'you want this as an apron?"

"Thanks." I smiled and tied it around my waist, then nudged Liam aside from the cash drawer. "I'll handle the money, if you like, and you and Jack can make the slushies."

"Yes, boss," Liam said, smiling at me. He turned to the green slushie machine. "Lucky I'm an expert."

As it turned out, neither Jack nor Liam were experts at all. Even though pouring slushies looked extremely easy and both of them were very smart, slush seemed to be going everywhere. With kids shouting their orders and more and more people joining the line, the pressure mounted. Jack spilled some slushie on Liam's shirt, then Liam "accidentally" spilled a slushie on Jack.

But Liam was being weirdly nervous around me. He was super careful not to spill any slushies on me. And even though Jack kept bumping into me in the confined space, Liam made sure he didn't. I wasn't sure if he was on edge because he liked me, or if he was trying to avoid me. But every time he came close, my arms tingled. I snatched glances in Liam's direction, noticing things about him that I hadn't seen before – the way his eyes lit up when he smiled, the way he bit his lip when he concentrated, the way his voice softened when he spoke to me.

I knew that I was falling for him, but I still wasn't sure if I should. We were friends, but did he think we were anything more than that? When there was a break in the line I grabbed my phone and slipped out of the trailer to check my texts.

Amazing here, Kimmi had texted. *You should see the house! Hanging out with Marco. Full report later.*

Is Saia there? Is he sad I didn't come? I asked.

Think I saw him. He was surrounded by about 10 girls so didn't have a chance to ask him! But I'm sure he's missing you.

Are they pretty? I texted back, a little disappointed to hear that Saia seemed to be having fun without me.

Not as pretty as you! How is Liam?

Fine, I think. But weird.

In a good way or a bad way?

Just a weird way. Full report later. Better get back to slushies.

Got to go too, Kimmi replied. *Annabel says hi. She's very busy with Ryan right now.* ☺

I watched Liam through the open trailer door. He and Jack were messing around and, for a moment, I wished things were easy between us, the way they were with him and Jack.

"Everything okay?" Liam called from the doorway to the trailer.

"Sure," I smiled, walking towards him. "Just checking on the girls. Kimmi says the party's amazing."

"Thanks for staying," he said softly. "I know you really wanted to go to the party."

"It's okay," I said. I really wanted to know what was going on behind those bright-blue eyes.

Liam turned to go back into the trailer, then seemed to change his mind. "Er, Phoebs," he said, in a serious tone.

My heart thumped. I was sure I could sense something important coming.

"Do you think –?"

That's as far as he got before Jack abruptly ended our conversation by pouring a slushie down the back of Liam's shirt. Way to ruin the moment!

"Cheap shot!" Liam shouted, shaking slushie out of his shirt and turning around to chase Jack with a mop.

Jack bounced around the trailer, howling with laughter.

By then a bunch of kids were shouting out orders. Liam put down his mop, Jack stopped laughing – eventually – and we all got back to work. I wondered what Liam had wanted to ask me. Was it something about *us*, or was it just a question about the Wild Club? It might have even been a question about slushies. But we got so busy I didn't have time to ask him.

By the time the slushie machines finally ran dry, Liam and I still hadn't had a chance to talk. The movie had finished without us seeing any of it, the floor was awash with multicolored slop and so were we. My dress was probably ruined forever. On the upside, we had made a pile of money for the orangutans. Polly came by to collect the money. She shook her head when she saw the state of the trailer and the color of our clothes, but she was pretty impressed by the amount of money in the cash drawer.

"Great work," she said. "Good luck with the cleanup!"

I looked around and sighed. I hated cleaning. "I don't remember signing up for this," I said.

"Sorry, princess," Jack said, handing me a dishcloth. "The servants have run away."

"Ha-ha." I started at one end of the counter.

Liam picked up the mop and Jack began cleaning the machines. As I was wiping down the counter, I heard my phone go off. I ignored it at first, but it went off again.

It was a message from Annabel with two words:

In love!

She'd sent a pic of her and Kimmi, with their

arms around Marco and Ryan. The four of them were pouting like models.

Everything went to plan? I texted.

Nearly had a disaster, Annabel replied. *I spied a Fairmount girl moving in on Marco. But I gave her the evil eye and she backed off.*

Well done! I replied. Kimmi would have been devastated if Marco had ended up with another girl.

How is the movie night going? Annabel asked.

Just cleaning up, I replied.

You know how to have fun! ☺

Sure do! Talk later. More fun cleaning to do!

I put my phone away and looked at the guys. Liam was mopping Jack's legs and Jack was trying to wipe Liam's face with his sticky cloth. This was going to take a while.

The field was almost deserted by the time we finally closed the door to the slushie trailer. The three of us wandered back through the school to the street in silence. The guys didn't live far away and were walking home, but I had to wait for my mum to pick me up.

I found a bench and sat down with a heavy sigh. It had been a long night. I was also disappointed that it was going to finish like this. I still didn't really know how Liam felt about me.

"I'll wait with you until your mum arrives, if you like," Liam said, sitting down beside me.

"Thanks," I said, smiling. "That'd be good."

Jack sat down next to Liam. A bit of shuffling went on and then Jack jumped to his feet again. "Ewww, I'm sticky all over. I think I'll go home and have a shower."

"Okay, dude," Liam said, giving him a friendly shove. "Why don't you do that?"

Jack gave Liam a fist bump. "I'm off," he said, and then disappeared into the darkness.

I glanced at Liam. I couldn't help thinking that Jack's departure hadn't been a coincidence, that Liam had asked Jack to leave us alone. I felt a little buzz of excitement run through my spine at the possibility that

I was finally going to find out what Liam wanted to ask me. We sat in silence for a few moments before Liam eventually spoke.

"So," he said quietly. "Glad you stayed to help out? Or are you sorry you missed the party?"

"I'm glad I stayed," I replied. It wasn't the important question I'd been hoping for, but it was a start. "We made some money for the Wild Club and it was great to see my film on the big screen. And it was pretty fun hanging out with you and Jack. Even though you spilled as many slushies as you sold."

"Well, Jack totally lost the slushie fight," Liam said, smiling. Then he shuffled his feet awkwardly and stared down the street. "Guess your mum'll be here soon."

"Yeah, soon," I said.

We sat in silence for what seemed like forever after that. And I began to wonder if Liam was actually going to ask me anything important. Maybe Jack really had just gone home because he wanted a shower. Liam had spilled slushies all over him, and then mopped his face and hair, after all. But as I watched Liam out of the corner of my eye, tapping his fingers on the bench, I knew I needed to find out what was going on in his head – and fast because Mum would be here any second.

"I was thinking we should go to the movies sometime," I said tentatively.

I watched Liam as the tapping stopped and his expression changed. A smile spread across his face. I knew I'd said the right thing. I still didn't know exactly what was going on in his mind, but I felt like I was getting closer.

"I was just thinking the same thing," Liam said. "Yeah, that'd be really cool."

"Maybe we could go tomorrow," I suggested.

Liam's face fell. "Sorry, not tomorrow."

"Oh," I said, wishing I hadn't pushed him.

"Not because I don't want to," he went on. "It's just – I'm going out with my parents."

"Family lunch?" I said. "Poor you."

Liam shook his head. "There's a pod of whales off the coast. My parents are going out tomorrow to take a look and I'm going, too."

"How cool," I said. "Sounds a lot more exciting than any family outing I've ever been on."

Liam's face brightened. "You want to come too?"

"Are you joking?" I asked.

Liam shook his head. "It's not a tourist boat. We'll be going out with a bunch of scientists. They never talk – except when it's about whales. Then they never stop."

I laughed. "Sounds like a perfect way to spend the day."

"Great," he said quietly. "It'll be fun."

Liam looked at me again with that intense expression that he'd been giving me all night, and I wondered if he was going to kiss me. But by then it was too late. Mum had pulled up beside us.

"You want a ride home?" I asked.

"Nah," Liam shook his head. "Jack won't be far away, I'll catch up with him."

"Okay, see you tomorrow," I said, getting into Mum's car.

Mum chattered to me all the way home, but I hardly heard what she was saying.

Tomorrow, I'll have all day to hang out with Liam again, I kept thinking. And who knows what might happen then!

Phoebe GOES TO meet *Saia*

Chapter Ten

Liam's hurt expression stayed with me the whole time as Kimmi's mum drove us to Ryan's party. Beside me, Annabel was bursting with excitement, but I just felt rotten about letting down my friends in the Wild Club. To make things worse, I'd rushed off so quickly, I hadn't even wished them good luck.

"Stop moping," Annabel said, noticing my mood. "You're going to have an amazing time. Forget Liam and start thinking about Saia."

"Right," I nodded, trying to push Liam's face out of my mind. "Saia." I pulled out my phone and reread his text, and his adorable smile came back to me.

"See?" Annabel said. "You're smiling already."

Kimmi turned around in the front seat to look back at me. "You can still be friends with Liam, even if things work out with Saia."

I nodded, but I wasn't so sure. Liam might be mad at me for a very long time. I was still thinking about the slushie stand as the car pulled up at Ryan's. But then I saw the *house*. Looming ahead of me was a grand stone building, three stories high and all lit up like electricity was free. "Wow," I said, climbing out of the car. "Are you sure this is the right place?"

"Uh-huh," Annabel said, getting out behind me. "Pretty impressive, huh?"

"Whoa," Kimmi sighed, as she joined us on the street and her mum drove away. "It's like a hotel or something."

"I think it's bigger," I said.

"Shh," Annabel hissed. "You sound like a pair of hillbillies who've never been out of your *sleepy li'l town*."

"Or a pair of Westway girls who've never been to a party at a harborside mansion before," I said. "What if I trip on a Persian rug and smash into an antique or something?"

"Don't be ridiculous," Annabel said. "Ryan's not going to have a party in a room full of antiques."

"Guess not," I laughed, but the house was so imposing, it was hard not to feel a little intimidated.

Annabel put her arm through mine, grabbed Kimmi with the other, and we headed for the house, where two big iron gates and one very large security guard stood between us and the party.

"Names, please," the guard said.

Annabel spoke for all of us and the guy ran his finger down a list, checking off Annabel and then Kimmi. My heart thumped as he scanned the list for my name, and I wondered for a moment if I'd really been invited.

"Right. There you are," he said, finally finding me. "Straight up the driveway and turn left. Just follow the music."

The security guard pressed a button and the gates creaked open, letting us in.

Kimmi giggled as we hurried up the driveway. "No way. I knew we were on a guest list but I didn't think there'd be a security guard with an *actual* list. It's like we're going to an exclusive nightclub!"

Annabel nudged her. "If you want to fit in, don't act so surprised about everything."

"Right," Kimmi nodded.

Then Annabel looked at me. "And stop fiddling with your dress. You look gorgeous."

"Oh, okay," I said. I hadn't even noticed I was fiddling. I wasn't worried about my dress either, until I saw the other girls standing at the top of the driveway. They were all beautiful – their dresses looked expensive, their hair shone and their faces glowed.

I tugged at my dress. I'd loved it a minute ago, but now it felt cheap. And so did I. I wasn't wearing make-up, and I probably still had paint in my hair. I looked at my flats. The other girls were all in heels. Why hadn't I spent more time getting ready?

"Those are the girls we saw at the rugby game," Kimmi mumbled, as we passed them. "What are they doing here?"

"Relax," Annabel said. "Stop stressing about everything. Come on."

We followed the noise and a trickle of guys to the back of the house and through a set of double doors into a huge room. It was like a giant cave, with strobe lights flashing in time to a throbbing beat. About a hundred guys and girls milled around in the flickering light, but it was hard to tell who was in there. The light distorted everyone's faces, and anyone at the far end of the room was almost completely hidden by a screen of smoke. A DJ seemed to be hovering in thin air above the crowd. I'd never seen anything like it. There was no chance I'd trip over an antique in here, but I might never find Saia, either.

"This is amazing." I yelled in Annabel's ear, so she could hear me above the music.

"Told you it would be!" She grinned and squeezed my hand. "Let's find the guys."

I grabbed Kimmi's hand and we pressed our way through the crowd. A few girls were swaying to the music, but most people were just hanging out, surveying the scene.

"Can you see them?" Kimmi shouted, when we got to the far end of the room.

I shook my head, peering through the smoke to see if I could recognize anyone. I couldn't see Marco, Ryan or Saia, but I did notice a guy staring at Kimmi.

"There's a guy over there," I said, nudging Kimmi. "He's looking at you like he knows you."

"Where?" Kimmi said, blatantly turning around.

"Black shirt, blond hair, ten o'clock," I said.

"Never seen him before," Kimmi said, just as he looked her way again. Kimmi quickly turned away. "Awkward!"

"He's actually pretty cute," Annabel said, staring right at him. "If things don't work out with Marco —"

"What do you mean? They're totes going to work out with Marco," Kimmi interrupted. "Let's see if the guys are outside."

Kimmi marched off into the crowd with Annabel and me right behind her. But we hadn't gone far when a bunch of girls bounced out of nowhere and smacked right into us, sending us tumbling into a huddle of guys. Kimmi seemed to lose her footing, and reached out for the nearest stable object, which happened to be the guy in the black shirt.

"Oops, sorry, my bad!" she apologized. Blushing, she quickly righted herself, then let go of the guy's arm and stepped back.

The guy spun around to face her, looking confused at first. Then he smiled, realizing who had bumped into him. "You okay?"

"Yeah, thanks. Just tripped, sorry." Kimmi's eyes darted from the guy to us. "Anyway, better go."

"Yeah, see you around," he called. "I'm James, by the way."

"I'm Kimmi. Hey, nice to meet you. Bye." Kimmi rushed off, grabbing my hand on the way past. "How embarrassing!"

"Chill out," Annabel laughed. "He was sweet."

Kimmi shook her head. "That was awkward. Let's just find the guys."

We shuffled our way across the room and then outside onto the terrace, breathing in the cool night air and taking in the view. I'd been in such a hurry to get inside when we arrived, I hadn't even noticed it. The terrace looked right across the harbor to the city.

"Not a bad place to live," I said, watching a ferry make its way across the river. I could definitely handle waking up to this view every day.

"Hey, you made it!" came a voice from behind us.

I turned around to see Saia. He had a gash above his right eye – from the rugby game, I guessed. It just made him look even cuter than ever. And his shirt was almost the same color as my dress. I felt my legs quiver when he smiled at me and said hello to the others.

"Have you just arrived?" he asked.

"Pretty much," I said.

"Any idea where Ryan is?" Annabel asked.

"And Marco?" Kimmi added.

Saia looked around. "They were right behind me.

Must have gone inside."

Annabel and Kimmi looked at each other, and before I had a chance to decide if I wanted to hang out with Saia on my own, they had disappeared, to look for the guys.

I smiled at Saia shyly, silently yelling at Annabel and Kimmi. I would have liked a little warning before being abandoned. What was I going to talk to him about? I could hardly think.

"So, looks like a great party," Saia said, fidgeting with a button on his shirt. Surprisingly, he looked almost as nervous as I felt.

"Yeah," I nodded. "Hard not to have a great party in a house like this, though. It's amazing. How many people actually live here?"

"Just Ryan and his brother – oh, and their parents, of course."

"Seriously?" I said. "It's so big. Wow!"

Saia laughed and I quickly shut my mouth, realizing that I had just done exactly what Annabel had told me *not* to do. I was acting really surprised about everything.

It was so much easier talking to someone via text. I looked at Saia, wondering what he thought of me. He was still smiling, so that was a good sign.

"I think my house would fit in that shed," Saia said, pointing to a small structure at the end of the yard. Surely that wasn't true, but it was sweet of him to say. Annabel was right – I did have to chill out more.

"That big? What luxury!" I laughed until I realized he might have thought I was mocking him. "Great game today," I said, quickly changing the subject. "We didn't see the whole thing. But that try you scored at the end? You smashed it."

Saia beamed. "Just a lucky break," he said modestly.

"Come on," I gave him a nudge. "You left that other guy for dead. You were a total star."

Saia couldn't help smiling, a broad grin spreading over his face. "Thanks. It's not like that every week. But it's kind of good when it is. What sports do you play?"

"Ah," I said, trying to think of something I did that passed as a sport, and coming up with nothing. "I'm on the debate team. Does that count?"

"You must be really smart."

"No, not at all," I laughed. "I'm just weird. Instead of playing sports at lunchtime like normal people, I go to debate meetings. I'm also in a club that raises money for endangered animals. Actually, there's a movie night fundraiser for orangutans at our school tonight."

I told Saia all about what we'd been doing in the Wild Club. Once I got started, it was hard to stop. I'd been going on about logging and habitat destruction for ages before I suddenly realized what I was doing. "Sorry, I'm probably boring you senseless."

Saia shook his head. "It's cool. Honestly. It sounds like you really care about this stuff. So why aren't you at the movie night, instead of here?"

I shrugged, suddenly feeling awkward. "We had already made plans to come to this party when I found out about the movie night. So … here I am," I said.

Saia smiled. "Well, I'm glad you came." He edged closer and I thought he might be about to kiss me, when suddenly he stiffened. Something behind me had distracted him.

I turned to look. In the shadows, beneath a big, sprawling tree, I could see a couple. From a distance, it looked like Marco and Kimmi. But when I looked more closely I could tell from the clothes that it wasn't Kimmi. I was almost certain the guy was Marco, though. He and the girl were so close, it definitely looked like something was going on. As I watched, she leaned towards Marco and kissed him.

"Oh, no," I groaned. "That's not good."

The tension that had built up between me and Saia unraveled completely. He looked down, like he was embarrassed. I didn't know where to look either. I couldn't stand the thought of Kimmi coming out here and seeing this.

"Who's that girl?" I asked.

"She's from Fairmount."

I looked at the girl again and recognized her from the rugby game. And she'd been standing at the top of the driveway when we arrived.

"You know her?" I asked.

Saia nodded. "Marco's been after her for ages."

"Oh," I said glumly. "Poor Kimmi. She thought she'd be hanging out with Marco tonight."

"Yeah, that's kind of awkward." Saia frowned.

"Really awkward. What am I going to say to Kimmi?"

Saia shrugged. "It's probably kinder if you don't say anything."

Maybe Saia was right. If I told Kimmi about the Fairmount girl, she'd have a total meltdown and want to go straight home. But then again, if I said nothing, she'd spend the whole night looking for Marco, wondering what was going on. I couldn't do that to her – it just seemed cruel.

"I think I should find Kimmi and make sure she doesn't see this," I said. I turned to go and walked straight into Annabel and Kimmi.

"Oh, hey!" said Annabel. "Here you are. Look who we found!" She nodded at Ryan, looking thoroughly pleased with herself.

Kimmi looked slightly lost. "Still can't find Marco," she said. "Maybe he's gone home."

I stared at Kimmi, wondering what to say. If she found out the truth, she'd be so upset she'd want to leave right away. Should I lie and tell her I didn't know where Marco was to protect her feelings? Or should I tell her the truth?

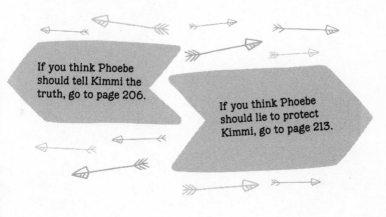

If you think Phoebe should tell Kimmi the truth, go to page 206.

If you think Phoebe should lie to protect Kimmi, go to page 213.

Phoebe CONFRONTS Annabel

Chapter Ten

"Phoebs, what about Liam?" Annabel asked again, staring at me.

I looked at my feet. I felt my throat constricting, but I knew I had to tell her what was bothering me.

"Liam texted me today," I said, my voice croaking. I cleared my throat. "He thinks I've got a boyfriend at Highgrove and I'm too involved with him to care about the Wild Club."

Annabel raised her eyebrows. "Why does he think that?"

"He said … you told him."

Annabel gasped. "I did not! Why would I do that?"

"I'm not saying you *did*," I said quickly. "I'm just repeating what he told me."

"I didn't say that. Why would I say you're not interested in the Wild Club, or that you've got a boyfriend?"

I looked at her carefully. She seemed genuine. "I know, right?" Annabel might have been a bit boy crazy, but she was still my friend. "It doesn't make sense."

Annabel shook her head. "I really don't know where Liam got that from."

"Me neither," I sighed. "Sorry, Annabel." I hugged her, remembering for the first time all week what a good friend she was. This whole thing with Liam had really caused a rift. I felt stupid for getting so jealous. "Friends?" I smiled.

"Best friends," Annabel said, smiling.

We both looked at Kimmi and put our arms out so she could join our hug, but she didn't move.

"Come on, Kimmi," Annabel called. "Group hug."

"There's something else Phoebe has to tell you," Kimmi said, still not moving. "About Liam."

I glared at Kimmi. We'd sorted things out. It was

time to move on, not reveal my feelings for Liam.

"If you don't tell her, I will," said Kimmi to me firmly.

I shook my head.

"Phoebe's in love with Liam," Kimmi announced.

"I am not!" I shrieked.

Annabel stared at me.

"I'm not!" I said. "We're friends. Just friends. That's all."

"*Phoebs*," Kimmi said. "Time for a full confession."

"There's nothing to confess," I insisted, smiling insanely at Annabel.

"Really?" Annabel asked. "You promise there's nothing between you two?"

I coughed, my throat getting tight again. I couldn't lie to her anymore. "Okay, the truth." I took a deep breath. "We *were* just friends. Well, that's what I thought. But after that day when we all went to the mall, I started to feel differently about him. And then things started going really well between you two … I got jealous. I mean, of course he likes you. Why wouldn't he?" I looked at my feet. "I'm not proud of it. But I was jealous because he likes you and not me. And that's why I didn't go to any of the meetings last week. I couldn't cope with seeing you and Liam together. Stupid, huh?"

I looked at Annabel, waiting for her reaction. She didn't say anything for a minute, but something seemed to soften in her expression. "Listen," I went on. "Just forget all about it. You and Liam should get together. I can just be his friend, like always. It's no big deal. I've been jealous and stupid."

"Oh, Phoebe," Annabel cried, squeezing my hands. There were tears in her eyes. "I feel awful. I never would have gone after Liam if I knew you really liked him."

I shrugged. "It's not your fault. I didn't even know myself, at first." I gave Annabel a hug. "What a mess."

"Yeah, it is," Annabel nodded.

"It's going to feel really small in that slushie stand tonight," Kimmi said. "Maybe I'll go to the party after all." She laughed, but nothing seemed funny.

"It'll be fine," Annabel said. She looked at me and smiled, then grabbed her things.

"It will?" I asked. "How?"

"I won't go to the movie night."

I stared at her, hardly able to believe what I was hearing.

"You and Kimmi go," Annabel went on. "I'll just go home."

"No!" I cried. "You should go. I'll just be in the way. I'll go home."

But Annabel pulled free of me and walked towards the bedroom door. "I'm not interested in Liam if he's going to come between you and me, Phoebs. I'm really sorry. I know how much the Wild Club means to you. You go."

"Wait!" I said, trying to grab Annabel's hand, but she stepped out of my reach and rushed down the hall.

"It's fine!" she called over her shoulder. "Have fun! Go Wild Club!" Then I heard the front door slam. She was gone.

"O-kay," I sighed, falling backward onto Kimmi's bed. "I didn't see that one coming. I feel really terrible now. Do you think I should run after her?"

Kimmi shrugged. "Weird, huh?" She stared at the doorway where Annabel had disappeared. "But I don't think there's any point chasing after her. You know what she's like when she's made up her mind."

I nodded. "She's so determined."

Kimmi fluffed up her hair and then packed the banner that she'd made with Jack. I checked the time. It was getting late. It seemed like the only thing we could do was get to school to help the guys with the slushie stand and let Annabel go. I felt sorry for her. I knew exactly how it felt to have your best friend like the guy you're crushing on. There was no point ruining our friendship over a guy. I could only be Liam's friend.

I was glad we'd cleared things up. But something was still playing on the back of my mind. If Annabel didn't tell Liam I had a boyfriend, why did he say she had? One thing was for sure – I was going to find out tonight.

People were already starting to trickle onto the field when we arrived. Groups of girls and guys gathered on the grass near the big screen. Couples spread blankets and unpacked their picnics. And on the bank above the field, I could see the slushie trailer, with Jack and Liam already serving a customer. We'd missed the set-up completely.

"So, when did you forget all about Marco?" I asked Kimmi as we walked towards the trailer.

Kimmi shrugged. "I've just been hanging out with Jack a lot, and it kind of crept up on me. Jack's much quieter than Marco, but he's got swag – he's so cool on a skateboard. He's also arty and interesting. And I think he likes me too."

I smiled. "Jack's a great guy. I really hope it all works out for you." It was good to see Kimmi move on from her obsession with Marco. It probably wasn't good for her confidence to be chasing a guy who didn't seem to notice her.

"Nice timing." Liam smiled when we climbed into the trailer. "All the hard work's done."

"Didn't want to get in the way," I joked. I watched him carefully. I'd expected Liam to be uptight, since he'd lied to me that afternoon, but he seemed completely relaxed. He was looking cuter than ever in his aqua shirt. His hair was pushed back off his face for a change, and his eyes seemed to stand out even more. *Friends*, I kept thinking to myself, determined to believe it. *We're just good friends.*

"What happened to Annabel?" Liam asked.

"Family crisis," Kimmi said. "She's really sorry she can't come."

I glanced at Liam to check his reaction, but he just shrugged. "Oh, well."

He seemed surprisingly chill about it, given how much time they'd spent together in the past week. He must have been good at covering up his feelings.

Beside me, Kimmi and Jack were looking very relaxed, too, as they unfurled the Slushies in Paradise banner. They chatted and laughed as they hung it over the counter. I could already see that they were going to make a great couple.

"What d'you think?" Kimmi said when the banner was in place.

I went outside to take a look. The sign was painted with trees. There were little orangutans hanging from the branches, and a sun setting over the whole scene.

"Really great," I said, admiring Jack and Kimmi's work.

"Beautiful," Liam agreed, joining me in front of the trailer.

But I noticed he wasn't looking at the artwork – he had his eyes on me. *Awkward.* Or maybe I was just imagining things.

"So, are you planning to do some actual work?" Liam said. "Or are you just here for show?"

I laughed. Liam was obviously mocking me. But I wasn't sure if it was because I was being lazy or because I was overdressed for the slushie trailer. Annabel's top and wedges were a big mistake. Luckily Kimmi had thought to grab aprons before we left her house. I went back into the trailer and tied one on to protect Annabel's top. I felt a pang of guilt. I was wearing her stuff and hanging out with the boy she liked while she was at home on her own. What kind of friend did that make me?

By then a line had formed outside the trailer. I had to get to work.

It didn't take long to work out that the trailer was only designed for two. Once it got busy, it was ridiculously crazy with four of us taking money, pouring slushies, leaning over each other and getting in each other's way. Even after we divided up the jobs so we didn't all need to be on the slushie machines, it was still chaos. Jack poured slushie all down my arm as I tried to fill a cup, and then I bumped into Liam with two full slushies, and one ended up going all over his shirt. Luckily he just laughed about it. Then he accidentally slopped slushie down my leg. That made me laugh at first, until it dripped onto Annabel's wedges.

"I think we need to work in shifts," I suggested.

"Love the plan," Jack said, wiping his hands on his shorts. "How 'bout you guys stay here, and we'll come back at intermission?" We all agreed, and Jack turned to Kimmi. "Coming?"

The movie, a romantic comedy, had just started on

the big screen. Kimmi shrugged casually and smiled, but I could tell she was jumping up and down on the inside. She'd be happy to snuggle up with Jack on the grass.

She hung up her grubby apron and smoothed out her dress, then followed Jack out of the trailer, turning to give me a big smile before she left. I felt so happy for her. I was glad things were working out with her and Jack.

I sighed. "Such a cute couple."

Liam nodded, but he wasn't looking. He was watching me again. I started thinking about how much I wanted to be snuggling up with Liam under the stars right now. But I didn't want to ruin my friendship with Annabel. If only I'd realized how gorgeous he was *before* Annabel joined the Wild Club.

"Five Borneo Sunsets," came a voice from the other side of the counter. I looked out to find the line growing again.

"I'll take the register, you can make the slushies, if you like," I said to Liam.

"Sure, whatever you want," he said, and started pouring slushies.

I sighed to myself as we got back to work. What I wanted was never going to happen.

I was totally wrecked by the time Kimmi and Jack returned to take over the slushie stand. The movie had been paused for an intermission, which meant we were crazy busy in the trailer. Kids were shouting, money was going everywhere and so were the slushies. Kimmi and Jack squeezed in beside us.

"I have to tell you something," Kimmi whispered.

"Three Rain Forest Greens and two Blue Lagoons," Liam said, sliding a stack of slushies onto the counter beside me.

Kimmi pursed her lips until Liam had his back turned again. It seemed like she had something important to share, but she wasn't going to get a chance while we were crushed in a trailer like this.

"Just need to go outside for a sec," I said loudly, as I climbed out of the trailer.

I nodded to Kimmi to follow, but before she had a chance, Liam came after me.

"Looks like it's our turn to enjoy the movie," he said.

"Oh yeah, right," I nodded, a wave of excitement sweeping over me, despite myself. I glanced over Liam's shoulder to see Kimmi at the slushie machine. She was mouthing something to me, but I had no hope of working out what she was saying. I guessed she had exciting news about her and Jack, but whatever it was, it would have to wait. For now, I had issues of my own to work out. I was just about to watch a movie with Liam. How was I going to act normally when I felt like I'd swallowed a packet of jumping beans?

"Do you prefer being close to the screen or back farther?" Liam asked, assessing the crowd on the field.

"Don't mind," I said, trying to sound calm. "Wherever we can squeeze in."

Friends, just friends, I said to myself as we headed towards the field. I put my hands in my pockets so I didn't accidentally brush against Liam. Even though I would have loved to be holding his hand, I knew I couldn't.

We found a spot on the edge of the crowd. He leaned towards me. "This okay?" he whispered, trying not to disturb the people around us.

I nodded. "Great."

But as we settled on the small patch of grass, things started to get not-so-great. Liam sat down so close to me, I could feel the warmth of his arm.

I turned my eyes to the big screen. But even though I tried to watch the movie, all I could think about was the guy sitting next to me.

Friends, just friends, I kept saying to myself. But by then my heart was thumping and it felt like my legs had melted into the grass. My head felt like it was drifting away like a helium balloon.

I tried to focus on the movie, pushing thoughts of Liam out of my mind. There was no point torturing myself with the fact that I liked Liam. He was off-limits – except as a friend.

I can do this, I thought. But then Liam ruined everything. He slipped his hand on top of mine.

I wriggled my fingers slightly, just in case it had been

an accident. But his hand didn't move. My whole body stiffened as I realized this was no accident. This was exactly what I had dreamed of, but it couldn't happen in real life. I didn't know what to do.

Should I stay here and watch the movie with Liam? Or should I go back to the slushie stand, and make sure we stayed just friends?

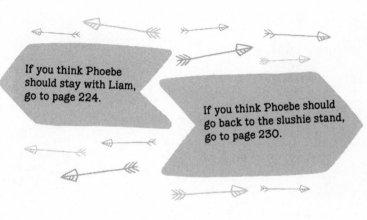

If you think Phoebe should stay with Liam, go to page 224.

If you think Phoebe should go back to the slushie stand, go to page 230.

Phoebe PRETENDS nothing is *wrong*

Chapter Ten

"Phoebs, *what* about Liam?" Annabel asked again, staring at me.

I glanced at Kimmi. She raised her eyebrows and nodded, urging me to tell Annabel about the text, but I didn't want to make the night any worse now that we were going to be side by side at the slushie stand.

"What is it?" Annabel asked again. "Something good, I hope?"

"Of course," I replied thinly. "I ... just wanted to tell you what a nice guy he is."

Annabel frowned. "I know."

"Yeah, but did you know he was down at the cove

last Saturday, cleaning up trash? He's really sweet."

"Oh, yeah, tell Annabel about the cove," Kimmi encouraged me.

"Why? What happened?" asked Annabel. "Liam didn't tell me about it."

"Oh, a funny story really. I was down there with him and I took some brownies."

"Hold on," Annabel interrupted. "Liam was at the skate park on Saturday."

I thought for a moment. "This was in the morning. Anyway, I took some brownies that Lulu made, and Liam ate one and he had to run off to throw up. Then I discovered that Lulu had put dog biscuits in them." I laughed. It seemed much funnier now.

Kimmi smiled too. But Annabel's mouth was set in a hard line. "Why were you at the cove with Liam, taking him brownies?"

I stopped laughing and looked at Annabel. "He asked me to come down and –"

"Like on a date," said Annabel.

"No, no," I said. "I went to help clean up the beach.

But we ended up building a sand mermaid with Lulu."

I watched Annabel's face fall and her shoulders collapse. She looked really disappointed that I'd been hanging out with Liam. I hadn't told her the story to make her feel bad. I was just trying to get out of a sticky situation, but things were getting even more awkward between us.

"Then what happened?"

I shrugged. "Nothing happened." At least that bit was true.

"Really?" she asked.

"Yes, really."

Annabel drew a deep breath and then looked at Kimmi. "Really?"

Kimmi threw her hands in the air. "Don't look at me. It's not my story."

I shuffled uncomfortably as Annabel sighed again. She seemed really upset.

"Suppose we should get going," Kimmi said. "The guys will be expecting us to set up."

She packed up the banner that she and Jack had

made. "Is everyone ready?"

Annabel and I glanced at each other warily. I still didn't know if Annabel had intentionally lied to Liam about me having a boyfriend or if there'd just been a mix-up, but it hardly seemed to matter. She was clearly hooked on Liam and she was doing everything she could to get him. I was just getting in the way. Annabel was usually so bubbly and happy, but right now she looked so sad I felt sorry for her. All the excitement I'd felt about helping on the slushie stand with Liam evaporated. I didn't want to upset Annabel, and I didn't want a guy coming between us. I dawdled behind my two friends as we headed for Kimmi's mum's car, trying to think of a way to get out of the movie night. I had to come up with an excuse.

"Oh, no," I cried suddenly, staring at a message on my phone. "There's been an emergency at home. I have to go."

The girls both turned to look at me. I waved my phone at Annabel and Kimmi, hoping they didn't look too closely. It was just an old message from Mum that I was showing them.

"What kind of emergency?" Kimmi asked.

"Not sure. Mum just said: *Come home now*. I can't believe it. What timing!" I huffed, pretending to be really disappointed about having to leave.

"Do you need a ride home?" Kimmi asked.

"No need," I said. "I'll walk back."

"Do you think you'll miss the whole night?" Annabel asked.

"Hope not, but I might have to," I sighed.

"Oh, that's a shame." Annabel sighed too, but I could tell she was faking, just like me. She must have been happy to see me going.

"Have fun!" I called, as I raced home. I didn't want to miss the movie night, but I didn't want Annabel hating me because she thought I was interfering. After a week of being jealous and bitter, I just wanted to be a good friend. If Annabel changed her mind about Liam, then I *might* do something about my feelings for him, but for now it was better to just go home.

I hadn't even reached my front door when Kimmi started texting me.

What are you doing? If you're not going to ask Annabel what's going on, I will.

No! I replied. *I'm over Liam. I want things to work out for Annabel. Have fun and I want a full report on you and Jack at the end of the night!*

Are you sure? Kimmi replied.

Yes! ☺ I texted back.

OK. I hope I have something to report!

Lulu was already in her pajamas and ready for bed when I got home. She looked very cute in her pink-spotted top and pants.

"You look yummy enough to eat," I said, sweeping her up and giving her a squeeze.

"Phoebe!" she said, giggling. "You can get some ice cream if you're hungry."

"I'm not hungry," I said. "How about I tuck you into bed and we can read a book." Reading to Lulu was always a great way to get over boy troubles.

"I'm not going to bed. I'm going for ice cream!" she cried.

"Phoebe, is that you?" came a voice from the kitchen.

"No it's a burglar," I called back. Lucky for everyone I wasn't. I could have walked right inside and taken anything.

"Back early?" Dad asked.

"Change of plans," I said.

"Oh, that's a shame. We were just coming down to see you."

"What – at the movie night?" I asked, feeling horrified.

Dad nodded. "I was going to take Lulu to get an ice cream from your stand."

A surge of red-hot embarrassment rippled through me. "Dad, why would you do that to me?"

"To help the orangutans," he said.

I shook my head. Dad could be so clueless. "No way! First, it's a *slushie* stand. And second, you're wearing a *bathrobe*!"

"It's a house coat," Dad corrected me, as if there was a difference.

"It's ugly, whatever it is."

"I want a slushie!" Lulu said excitedly.

"Sorry, Lulu," I said. "Not tonight."

She looked at me and screwed up her face like she was going to cry. But I knew what was coming. Lulu opened her mouth and screamed.

The movie had already begun when I arrived on the field with a large blanket, my sister, and her favorite teddy. As I knew very well, there was no point trying to negotiate with a four year old. I endured her screaming for about thirty seconds before I gave in and agreed to take her for a slushie. Thankfully Dad had just dropped us off and not humiliated me by coming along to the movie night.

"This looks like a nice spot," I said, putting Lulu down. She had insisted on being piggybacked from the car because she was wearing slippers.

I spread out the blanket and sat down with Lulu. "Okay, are you going to lie down and watch the film?"

"Can I have a slushie, *please*?"

"Lovely manners, Lulu," I said, smoothing out the blanket. "But the line is very long right now. We'll go soon."

With any luck my little sister would lie down, be soothed by the movie and fall asleep within seconds. Then there'd be no need to embarrass myself by going to the slushie stand at all. I crossed my legs and stretched out my arms.

"Come on, Lulu, you can sit with me."

Lulu smiled and snuggled in. For three or four lovely seconds she settled against my chest. Then she jumped up again. "I think the line is short now."

I pulled her back into my arms and whispered a rhyme as I stroked her hair. Before long I could feel her bouncy little body relax and then her breathing got deeper and finally I could see her eyes close. I settled back to watch the movie.

Lulu stirred every time the crowd laughed, but it was only during intermission, when people started talking and moving around, that Lulu fully came back to life. She immediately jumped to her feet and demanded a slushie. I knew if I tried to put her off again she'd throw a tantrum. So I got to my feet, grabbed Lulu's hand and reluctantly headed for the slushie trailer.

I could see only Liam and Jack in the slushie trailer as Lulu and I joined the line. I had hoped to avoid talking to Liam, but that wasn't going to be possible.

"Hey, Phoebe," Liam said, when I reached the front of the line. "I thought you had a family emergency."

I picked up Lulu so he could see her over the counter.

"A rainbow slushie, please," she said.

"Oh," Liam laughed. "There's your emergency. One rainbow slushie coming up."

"What happened to you?" I asked, as Liam turned to pour the slushie. "Looks like you've had a fight with a slushie machine." Liam's shirt was covered in bright-green syrup and his hair seemed to have a strange orange tinge to it.

"Ah," he smiled coyly, handing over Lulu's slushie and taking my money. "An accident."

"So, where are Annabel and Kimmi?" I asked, looking around. Jack was busy serving another customer but there was no sign of the girls.

"I think they're still in the bathroom."

"Oh, being lazy are they?" I laughed.

Liam rolled his eyes. Before I had a chance to ask any more, I was jostled aside.

"Five Blue Lagoons," came a voice from beside me.

"See you later!" I called to Liam.

I left Liam to get back to work and led Lulu away with her slushie, towards the bathroom. Something about the way Liam had rolled his eyes made me want to find Annabel and Kimmi.

I waited until Lulu had slurped down the last of her slushie and then poked my head inside the bathroom. There was a handful of girls at the mirror. At the far end of the room, Kimmi was standing outside a stall, whispering at the door.

"Annabel, please," I could hear her say.

I gave her a wave and she rushed over to meet me. "Phoebs!" she said, giving me a hug. Then she noticed Lulu. "Oh, you weren't lying about the family thing. Hey, Lulu."

"Long story," I said. "What's up with Annabel?"

"Liam said something to her," she whispered. "She got mad, and threw a slushie over him."

I put my hand over my mouth, trying to stifle a smirk. No wonder Liam looked like he'd been in a fight with a slushie machine. "What did he do to deserve that?"

"I don't know. She ran off without telling me. Now she won't come out of the stall."

"Poor Annabel," I whispered. "He must have said something horrible."

I wondered if I'd misjudged Liam. He didn't seem like the type to insult people. But maybe I didn't know him as well as I thought.

"Give me a few minutes. I'll see if I can talk her out of there."

I left Lulu with Kimmi and went to the stall where Annabel was holed up.

"Annabel," I whispered, gently knocking on the stall door. "What's up?"

"Why are you here?" she huffed.

"I brought Lulu to get a slushie," I said. "You want to come out and talk?"

I waited for a few minutes before I knocked again. "You can't stay there all night."

"I can," she snapped.

"I've got a blanket on the field. We can go and sit together and watch the end of the movie."

"No, I'm going to stay here."

I sighed, turned around and leaned my back against the door. "How about I pour another slushie on Liam's head for you. Will that help?"

"Maybe," Annabel replied.

"Or I could make him another batch of brownies. This time I could put curry powder in them."

"Yeah, that'd be good," Annabel replied.

"Or I could be really mean and make them with whole chilies. That'll teach him for upsetting you."

Annabel sniggered.

"So, you want to come out?"

"No," Annabel replied.

"Any luck?" Kimmi asked, as she and Lulu came to join me.

I shook my head. "I don't know what to do," I sighed.

Then I noticed Lulu was down on the floor, poking her head under the door.

"*Lulu,*" I hissed. But she just ignored me.

"Annabel, are you sad?" Lulu asked in her unmistakable style. "I like to sing when I'm sad. Would you like me to sing to you?"

Before Annabel had a chance to answer, Lulu had begun a lively rendition of *Twinkle Twinkle Little Star.*

A few moments later the door opened and Annabel finally emerged, with Lulu still singing. Lulu sure knew how to create a problem but, every now and then, she also managed to solve one. Annabel looked at Kimmi and me, then smiled as Lulu grabbed her hand and led her to the sinks.

"Don't forget to wash your hands," Lulu instructed.

"All right, Little Miss Bossy," Annabel laughed.

Outside the bathroom, we all gave Annabel a hug and then sat down. Lulu curled up on my lap.

"What did Liam say to you? I really thought he was a sweet guy. I can't believe he's upset you like this."

Annabel looked at me and sighed. "He didn't say anything."

I shook my head, confused. "So why did you throw a slushie at him?"

"I thought he was going to ask me out or something," she huffed. "But he was just messing around with Jack all night. He hardly paid me any attention at all."

"So you thought throwing a slushie at him would get you noticed?" Kimmi asked.

"No, I was just mad at him."

"And then you locked yourself in the stall because … ?"

Annabel looked at me forlornly. "Because I was mad at myself. I've been so stupid. Liam likes *you*. Not *me*."

"What?" I said, totally confused. "But I thought you said it was going really well with Liam."

"I made it up," Annabel said. "I wanted it to be true, but it's not."

I frowned. It didn't make any sense.

"I also kind of hinted that you had a boyfriend."

"Why?" I asked, getting mad.

Annabel stared at the ground. "You said you only wanted to be friends with him. And I really liked him, and I wanted him to like me too."

I could feel my blood boiling as she admitted lying to Liam. How could she have done that to me?

"But I really like Liam!" I said.

Annabel looked at me, her mouth hanging open. "You told me you were just friends. You said you'd *never* be more than that."

"I didn't say that," I said.

"Er, yes, you did," said Kimmi.

I stared at Kimmi. Whose side was she on? Annabel had been totally out of line, telling Liam that I had a boyfriend so he wouldn't be interested in me. That was just nasty.

"Can we build a sand mermaid tomorrow?" came a little voice from my lap.

I looked down. "Sure," I said, stroking Lulu's hair.

"We can go to the cove in the morning."

"And Kimmi can come?" she asked.

I nodded.

"And Annabel?" Lulu went on.

I looked at Annabel. I wasn't sure I was ready to spend the morning with her.

Then I noticed tears welling in her eyes. "I'm sorry, Phoebs," she said. "I've been so stupid. I really didn't know you liked him."

"I know you didn't," I said, but I still felt hurt.

Kimmi nudged me. "You know, Annabel kind of did you a favor. You really like Liam and he likes you. Neither of you would know that if Annabel hadn't got in between you."

I sighed. Kimmi had a point. I'd had no idea how much I liked Liam until Annabel had joined the Wild Club. And then I realized something else: I was a victim of my own lies as much as Annabel's. If I'd told her the truth about my feelings last weekend, things might have turned out differently.

I squeezed Lulu's hand. "Of course Annabel can

come to the cove, if she wants to."

Annabel nodded. "Sounds cool."

"No more secrets," Kimmi said, looking from Annabel to me. "Promise?"

We both nodded.

"You need to put a magic spell on it, if you want your promise to last," Lulu said, sitting up. She got to her feet and made us all join hands.

"Besties are the best,

Forget all the rest,

If you want a test,

Go and eat an ice cream sundae,

With sprinkles and marshmallows."

"So, friends are better than ice cream sundaes?" Annabel laughed.

Lulu thought hard about that. "Yes. Well, maybe."

"I guess there's one way to find out," said Kimmi. "Anyone up for a late-night feast?"

"Me!" Lulu squealed, jumping up and down in the middle of our circle. She grabbed my hand and started dragging me away. "Let's go home and make an ice cream sundae!"

I raised my eyebrows. It seemed risky to put Lulu in charge of food, but it was good to see everyone smiling again. When things calmed down I'd talk to Liam, and hopefully we could work things out, but for now I was just glad that Kimmi, Annabel and I were all best friends again. And eating an ice cream sundae seemed like a good way to prove it!

Phoebe TELLS Kimmi *the truth*

Chapter Eleven

"Um, Kimmi, I know where Marco is," I told Kimmi.

"You've seen him?" she said brightly. She obviously had no idea what I was about to tell her. I put my arm around her and led her away from the guys, making sure that she had her back to Marco. Annabel followed us. "You're not really going to like what I'm about to tell you," I warned her gently.

The smile slipped from her face. "What do you mean?"

I gave her a hug and then took a deep breath. I hated having to tell her that the guy she'd been dreaming about was with someone else.

"He's with another girl," I said eventually.

"What?" Kimmi said quietly. Her face went pale, and tears welled in her eyes. I felt awful, like I was the one who'd betrayed her.

"Oh, Kimmi," I said, squeezing her tight.

Annabel's eyes were darting around the terrace. Then her head suddenly jerked towards the trees. "No way," she mumbled, staring straight at Marco. "That dirtbag."

Kimmi's body stiffened and she spun around, following Annabel's gaze. "Marco?" she whispered.

"Forget him," I said, trying to steer Kimmi away, but she seemed determined to see for herself. Marco, on the other hand, hadn't even noticed he was the center of attention.

"It's one of the Fairmount girls," Kimmi mumbled. "The one we saw at the rugby game."

"It doesn't matter," I said, putting my arm around her. "Come on, let's go inside. Forget about him. He doesn't deserve you, Kimmi."

Kimmi shook her head. "I just want to go home."

"Okay," I agreed, sighing inwardly. "Sure, we can call Annabel's mum, we'll see if she can pick us up early."

Kimmi nodded. "Sorry, I know you were having fun. But I just can't stay here with them."

I turned to look at Saia. He was still behind us, with Ryan. I hated to leave him when we'd been getting along so well, but I had to take Kimmi home. I'd be seriously crushed, too, if I'd turned up and found Saia with another girl. I looked around for Annabel, but she was no longer beside me – she was marching towards Marco. What was she planning to do? Nothing she could say now was going to help Kimmi.

"Annabel," I called after her.

She turned and waved to us. "Come on," she said. "We're gonna sort this out."

Kimmi and I scurried after Annabel. It wasn't until the three of us were standing right in front of Marco that he and the Fairmount girl finally looked up. Annabel fixed Marco with a killer stare. It was enough to scare me, but he didn't even seem to notice.

"Hey, neighbor," Marco said to Annabel, as if he was chatting to her over the fence.

"Don't *hey neighbor* me," Annabel replied sharply.

Marco looked indignant and got to his feet. The girl he was with shuffled out of the way. She seemed to sense that Annabel was not someone to be messed with.

"You might remember Kimmi?" Annabel went on. "You've been leading her on all week. And now you're making out with some other girl. What's that about?"

Marco frowned. "I wasn't leading anyone on," Marco said, avoiding Kimmi's gaze. "And don't forget, I was the one who got you an invite. Westway girls don't normally come anywhere near parties like this. You should be thanking me, not mouthing off at me. You owe me."

I squirmed at the insult, and I could almost feel the steam coming out of Annabel's ears.

"Who do you think you are?" Annabel growled. If I was Marco right now, I'd be worried.

Marco backed away, but Annabel took a step towards him. "You think you're too good for us," she said angrily. "Well, I've got news for you, *neighbor*: my friend is way too good for *you*! So stay away from her."

"Whatever," Marco said, backing off.

I watched him leave, proud of the way Annabel

had stood up for Kimmi. "Way to go, girlfriend!" Even Kimmi managed a smile, though she still looked shaken.

"What a loser," Annabel said, shaking her head.

I turned to face Marco's friends, wondering what they'd made of the scene. Would they be mad at us for humiliating Marco? Ryan and Saia looked away, as if they were feeling uncomfortable. Were they embarrassed about us, or Marco? We stood awkwardly for a few moments, then Ryan grabbed Annabel's hand. "You want to go inside?"

"Good plan," Annabel said, grabbing Kimmi and dragging her along too.

I looked at Saia and he took my hand. I felt goose bumps spring up along my arm as we followed the others inside. The party was really pumping now and before long we were all swept up by the throbbing beat. I couldn't keep my eyes off Saia as we danced. The way his shirt matched my dress, it was almost like we were meant to be together. Every time he looked at me, I thought about kissing him. I wished I'd asked Annabel for some kissing advice, but it was too late now –

she was way too busy dancing with Ryan. Kimmi was on the other side of me. The guy in the black shirt had found his way over and was edging closer. She didn't seem to mind so much now.

I turned back to Saia – his face was so close I could feel the heat from his body. My heart was thundering in my chest. Then the strobe lights suddenly stopped flashing. Everyone shrieked as the whole room went black. I knew this was it.

I leaned towards Saia and closed my eyes. His lips met mine, like we'd been thinking the exact same thing. As we kissed, the entire world seemed to stand still. My mind soared to the ceiling and it felt like a thousand fizzy stars were dancing on my lips.

My first kiss was nothing less than perfect.

Phoebe LIES TO protect *Kimmi*

Chapter Eleven

"Yeah, I think Marco's gone home," I told Kimmi, praying she wouldn't notice him behind me.

I glanced at Saia, hoping he would understand what I was doing. Thankfully, he nodded.

"Wasn't looking too good when we arrived," Saia said. "Got a pretty bad knock at the game today."

I shot a grateful smile at Saia. He seemed to know I was trying to protect my friend.

Kimmi frowned. "But he's not answering my texts or anything. Hope he's okay."

"He's fine," Ryan laughed. "No brain, no pain."

"Harsh," Annabel giggled. "But probably fair."

"Should we go back inside?" I suggested, eager to get away before Annabel and Ryan said the wrong thing and ruined my plan.

Kimmi opened her mouth, but I grabbed her hand before she had a chance to reply and led her inside. With any luck, Marco and the Fairmount girl would stay outside and Kimmi would never find out what was happening. I'd break the news to her tomorrow. She'd be crushed, but at least she wouldn't be humiliated in front of a hundred people.

Inside, the music was thumping and everyone was bobbing around in a big seething mass. The party was getting wild. Annabel wiggled her way into a gap in the crowd and soon we were all bouncing along to the beat. I watched Saia's face as we danced, letting myself get swept along with his smile, and before long I was thinking about kissing him. I wished I'd asked Annabel for some advice on that, but she was way too busy with her arms around Ryan now. I turned to check on Kimmi, but she was no longer beside me. I glanced around, thinking she'd been swept off by the crowd, but I couldn't see her anywhere. I spun around, feeling terrible. I was supposed to be looking out for her, but I'd forgotten her completely.

"You seen Kimmi?" I asked Saia.

He looked around and shook his head. "Do you want some help to find her?"

"No, thanks," I said. If Kimmi was crying in the corner somewhere, I didn't think she'd want a guy around to see her. "I'll take Annabel. See you back here?"

Saia nodded and I gave him a little wave, then grabbed Annabel's hand, and led her out through the crowd.

"Hey," she said, when we reached the terrace. "What's going on?"

"Kimmi's gone. We have to look for her."

"Ryan was just about to kiss me!"

"Sorry, but I think Kimmi's looking for Marco," I explained. "Problem is, he's with another girl."

"What?" Annabel gasped. "You saw him?"

I nodded. "I didn't say anything because I wanted to protect Kimmi." But then I realized something: I hadn't only been thinking of Kimmi when I decided to lie about Marco. I'd been thinking of myself. I knew if Kimmi found out, she'd want to go home, and that would spoil things with Saia. I pulled out my phone to text her. "Oh, no," I sighed. "I've missed ten texts from her."

I scrolled through them, feeling worse and worse. Just as I thought, she'd gone to look for Marco, and found him – under the tree with the Fairmount girl.

I can't stay, her last message said. *I've called Mum. She's coming to pick me up.* ☹

"What a dirtbag," Annabel growled, looking around for him.

I put my phone away and thought for a moment. I couldn't bear the idea of Kimmi going home on her own, and there was still a chance we'd catch her before her mum arrived. "Quick, let's see if she's out in front."

We raced down the driveway to the street. It was quiet, except for a dog barking. I spotted Kimmi slumped against the fence.

"Kimmi!" I called.

She turned and gave us a slow, sad wave as we ran towards her. "I saw Marco with another girl," she cried.

Annabel threw herself at Kimmi, giving her a massive hug. "What are you doing? You don't have to leave just because Marco's a loser."

Kimmi shrugged. "Yeah, I do. But you stay. Have fun."

Annabel and I looked at each other. I knew she wanted to stay just as much as I did, but we couldn't abandon Kimmi when she needed us most.

"Of course we're coming with you," I said. "We'll just race back and tell the guys we're going."

Kimmi shook her head. "Don't let Marco ruin your night, too. Just stay with Saia and Ryan."

I grabbed Annabel's hand. "We'll be right back."

We were just about to rush off when Kimmi's parents pulled up beside us.

"Hello, girls," her mum called out the window. "How was the party?"

Kimmi opened the back door and climbed in. "Bad," she grumbled.

I looked at Kimmi, knowing what would happen if we ran off now. I really wanted to say good-bye to Saia, but there wasn't time. Instead, I sent him a quick text explaining what was happening, then climbed into the back of the car, pulling Annabel in with me. As we drove off, I turned and watched Ryan's house disappear behind us, feeling hollow. It was like I was leaving a little bit of my heart at the party.

"So, what happened tonight?" Kimmi's dad asked. "I thought you girls were planning to stay at Annabel's."

"Nothing happened," Kimmi replied flatly.

"Nothing at all?" her mum asked.

"*Nothing*," Kimmi repeated. "Now, you two just talk to each other because we've got private things to discuss in the back."

"I see," Kimmi's mum said.

Kimmi looked like she was about to cry.

"I can't believe Marco did that to you," Annabel said. "That's the last time I'm ever talking to him."

"I know," Kimmi said. "I can't believe it either. But I saw it all for myself. He was actually kissing that girl. I had to get out of there."

"Who was kissing?" Kimmi's mum interrupted.

"No one!" Kimmi snapped. "This is private."

"Fine, be like that," her mum said, and pumped up the volume on the radio. Some completely random old people's music was on.

"Mum, no!" Kimmi screeched.

But her mum pretended not to hear. Then things got worse – her dad started singing along. He sounded even worse than my dad. Kimmi protested, but that just made him sing louder, and then her mum joined in.

"You spin me right round, baby right round, like a record baby …"

I'd heard donkeys with better singing voices.

"So embarrassing." Kimmi glared at her parents.

I couldn't help smirking. It was definitely painful to listen to, but it was also pretty funny. Beside me, Annabel was dancing in her seat. When I nudged her, she started singing, too. It wasn't even the real song – just something she was making up as she went along.

"Marco is a dirtbag, baby, dirtbag. He is such a slime ball, what a lo-ser …"

I looked at Kimmi, raising my eyebrows. She

shrugged and put her arm around me. We both joined in. *"Marco is a dirtbag, baby, dirtbag …"*

It looked like Kimmi was beginning to have fun, but as soon as we finished singing, she got sad again.

"You're better off without him." I squeezed her hand, trying to console her.

She nodded. "But it still hurts."

"I know what will make you feel better," Kimmi's mum said, interrupting again. "A chick flick! We can all snuggle up on the sofa and watch a movie."

"Mum!" Kimmi protested. "Stop listening in! I'm fine, and I don't need to snuggle with you on the sofa. I'm not three."

"It's not a bad idea though," I whispered.

Annabel nodded. "Popcorn, a movie, a box of tissues. You'll be over Marco by midnight."

Kimmi smiled. "Sounds cool. So long as Mum doesn't join in."

As Kimmi and Annabel talked about which movie we could watch, my phone buzzed with a message. I quietly checked it, hoping that it was from Saia. I wondered what he thought of me disappearing with Kimmi and Annabel. I was pretty sure he'd understand, but my fingers trembled as I opened the message, I was so nervous. Sure enough, it was from Saia.

Sorry you had to go, he said. *Do you want to meet up tomoz? How about the cove?*

My heart jumped as I read it. *Sure thing*, I replied.

Annabel saw me texting and leaned across, peering at my phone. "You're meeting Saia tomorrow?"

I glanced at Kimmi, who looked hurt. "But I thought we could do something together," she whimpered.

"We will," I said. "We can all go to the cove."

"With you and Saia, all loved up?" she said forlornly. "That'll be fun."

I thought for a moment and then sent another message to Saia. *Annabel and Kimmi want to come too.*

Saia replied right away. *Cool. I'll bring Ryan and James. James says he met Kimmi at the party.*

I held my phone out so Kimmi and Annabel could read it.

Annabel started bouncing up and down right away,

but Kimmi frowned. "James? The guy that I fell on?"

"Guess that's the one," I smiled. "Cool, huh?"

"But I don't even know him," Kimmi moped. "What if we have nothing in common?"

"As long as he's nothing like that dirtbag Marco, it should be fine," Annabel said.

"And besides," I added. "It doesn't matter if you're different. Don't they say opposites attract?"

A tiny smile flickered across Kimmi's face. "They say that, do they?"

I grinned at Kimmi and Annabel. "They do. And you know what? They might just be right!"

The End

Phoebe STAYS WITH Liam

Chapter Eleven

I let myself enjoy the feel of Liam's hand on mine for several glorious moments – long enough to know that I didn't want to be just friends with him. I knew for sure how much I liked him, and now I could see he was into me, too. But while I wanted to stay like this forever, I kept thinking about Annabel. What would happen on Monday when I saw her? Or the next time I saw Liam at the Wild Club? How was that going to work out? I gently slipped my hand out from under Liam's and put it in my lap.

"There's something we need to talk about ..." I began, unsure what to say after that.

"Sorry, I shouldn't have …" he paused. "You *do* have a boyfriend at Highgrove, don't you?"

"No," I whispered indignantly. "That's not it. It's because of Annabel."

"*Annabel?*" Liam asked, a dumb look on his face.

I nodded. "Yes, that's the one. Long blond hair, bubbly, pretty."

"Yeah," he said, without smiling. "I know who she is. But what's she got to do with anything?"

Now it was my turn to stare at him with a dumb look. "What do you mean?"

"She's just a friend. Annabel and I aren't together," Liam said firmly.

I turned and stared at the big screen, confused. "You've been hanging out with her all week," I said, trying to work out the truth.

Liam nodded. "Working on the stand. It doesn't mean we're an item."

"What about the skate park? You invited her skating. I saw her. She was wearing your helmet."

Liam shook his head. "I didn't invite her. She just

turned up. I thought she just wanted to learn to skate."
He pulled his phone out of his pocket. "You want to check my messages? See if you can find anything incriminating?"

I looked at his phone and then shook my head. I didn't want to trawl through his messages.

"Okay, here's one from yesterday," Liam went on. "Annabel asked me what time we were setting up. And this is how I replied." He showed me the screen.

Setting up at 5, it said.

That was it. There was no "love" or kisses or smiley face. It was actually pretty abrupt. It seemed like Liam was telling the truth.

"Why did Annabel tell me that things were going well with you, then?"

Liam shrugged. "I guess she wanted you to think they were. She also said you had a boyfriend."

"But she told me she didn't say that!"

"Well, okay. She didn't say that exactly. I just thought maybe you did because I saw you become friends online with this Highgrove guy called Saia, and when I asked

Annabel about it she hinted you were together. And when you didn't turn up to any meetings this week, she said you were too busy. I figured you didn't want to hang out with me anymore."

I swallowed hard as Liam's eyes searched my face for a response. "I don't even know Saia, I just got invited to a party he's going to. And I've only been skipping the Wild Club because I've been jealous of you and Annabel."

"You were … jealous?" he smiled shyly. "But Annabel told me you thought we'd never be more than friends." He kicked at the grass with his toe. "Did she make that up too?"

"Yes," I said. But it was a lie. I had said those exact words at the mall, right before Annabel started her campaign to get Liam. "Well, no. She didn't make it up. What I meant was I *thought* we were just friends, and then …" I dropped my gaze. How was I going to explain that my feelings for Liam had changed as soon as Annabel started flirting with him? "Things change," I said eventually.

And I realized that was true. Annabel hadn't exactly been honest with me or Liam. But I hadn't been honest with her about my feelings either. As soon as she found out the truth, she had stayed at home alone instead of coming between me and Liam.

"What does that mean?" asked Liam.

I took a deep breath. I could feel every hair on the back of my neck stand on end as Liam watched me, waiting for an answer. And I could have tried to explain everything, but it just felt right to show Liam how I felt. Enough words had been wasted in the past week, saying things that weren't true. I leaned towards him and gently kissed him on the lips.

"I'd like it if we could be more than friends."

"Oh," he smiled. "I'd like that too."

Phoebe GOES BACK to the *slushie stand*

Chapter Eleven

"Sorry, I think I'd better go," I mumbled, getting to my feet.

I raced between movie-goers and then ran for the slushie stand. I could feel my heart thumping as I ran. Why was Liam playing handsies with me when he was into Annabel? I must have misjudged him completely.

I desperately needed to talk to Kimmi.

When I approached the slushie trailer, I saw Kimmi and Jack leaning on the counter, chatting. I hung back in the shadows, watching them. The customers had gone and they were smiling and laughing, obviously getting along well. I was sorry to break up the fun.

"*Kimmi!*" I called. I waved, gesturing for her to come out of the trailer.

"Phoebs, what's up?" she asked, bouncing towards me. Her face broke into a smile. "Did he ask you out?"

"No," I frowned. "Why would he do that?"

"Jack told me that Liam was going to ask you out."

I sat down on a bench and stared at Kimmi blankly. "What about Annabel?"

Kimmi sat down beside me and rolled her eyes. "There's nothing going on between him and Annabel. He likes you! That's what I was trying to tell you earlier."

I should have been excited, but I was still confused.

"But Annabel has been talking about Liam all week, and she said they were getting along really well. Do you think she was just making all that up? And the stuff about me having a boyfriend – what was that about?"

Kimmi shrugged. "Well, he was asking a lot of questions about you in the Wild Club meetings. Maybe she saw he was into you and she was trying to get him to like you less."

"By lying about me? By torturing me? If she

were here right now, I'd pour a slushie over her head. We're meant to be friends!" I couldn't understand why Annabel would do that to me.

Kimmi put her arm around me. "I don't think she was trying to be mean. She had no idea how you felt. Remember, you said that you and Liam would never be anything more than friends?"

"I didn't say …" I began. Then I remembered. "Oh yeah, I did say that."

"You also told Annabel that you didn't have a problem with her hanging out with Liam," Kimmi reminded me gently.

"Yes, but I didn't *mean* that. And I told her the truth tonight. And what did she do?"

Kimmi just looked at me.

"Oh, right," I mumbled. "She gave me her top and wedges and then went home."

Kimmi nodded. "She must have done that so you could work things out with Liam."

I sighed, feeling awful. I could hardly be angry at Annabel. I'd lied as much as she had. "Poor Annabel.

She's probably at home crying her eyes out because Liam doesn't like her."

"I feel bad for her," Kimmi added, checking her phone. A message had popped up.

"Timing. It's from Annabel and she's asking about you."

"What's it say?" I asked nervously.

Kimmi read the message out loud. "*How is Phoebs? She hasn't replied to my messages. Tell her I'm sorry I lied about what happened with Liam. She should go for him. They'll make a cute couple.*"

Kimmi looked at me and raised her eyebrows. "It's a confession."

"And an apology," I said, unsure how to react.

A great big mixture of emotion was swimming around inside me. I felt hurt, guilty and excited, all at the same time.

I needed to get my phone to message Annabel, but I also had to apologize to Liam for rushing off.

I looked over towards the slushie trailer, where I could now see Liam with Jack, cleaning up. This was going to be awkward, but at least I'd worked out the truth now. I wondered how Annabel would react if Liam really did ask me out. Even though she'd told me to go for him, she'd probably still be a little bit upset. I would have to be careful if I was going to hang out with Liam – I wanted to stay friends with Annabel.

"No way!" Kimmi shrieked. She was staring at her phone.

"What?" I asked.

Kimmi showed me a picture. It was Annabel and her old crush, Ryan Baker, with their arms around each other.

I laughed. "Poor Annabel," I said, shaking my head. "I'm really worried about her. She looks heartbroken, doesn't she?"

"I guess she's over Liam, then," Kimmi giggled. "I can't believe she went to Ryan's party alone – and she's hanging out with him! I think you can stop feeling sorry for her," said Kimmi. Then she leaned in close to me and whispered, "You know, Jack says Liam has liked you for ages."

"Hey, Phoebe!" someone called. I turned around

and saw Liam heading towards me. "You're missing the movie. Is everything okay?"

I walked right up to him. "Yes," I said. "It couldn't be better."